MISTLETOE ON THE RANGE

RED HART RANCH

SOFIA AVES

First Edition

EBOOK ISBN 978-1-923471-17-7

PRINT ISBN 978-1-923471-18-4

RHR READING ORDER

Rhys Archer and Eve Beaumont hero several books, crossing series from Red Hart Ranch to Texan Devils. Their story continues in a linear order with critical information in each. Their reading order is listed below, along with Will Kirk's, if you haven't read both full series in order.

ARCHER & EVE SUGGESTED READING ORDER
Snow on the Range
Ranger's Wrath
Mistletoe on the Range

WILL KIRK SUGGESTED READING ORDER
Ash on the Range
Kicking up Dirt
Kicking up Dust

CONTENT WARNING

Red Hart Ranch has had a sense of brutal beauty, but it's never been a place of perfect serenity. As the final book in this series, MISTLETOE ON THE RANGE covers lots of topics that may distress some readers. Please check the list below carefully.

- Murder
- Grief
- Death
- Parental loss
- Prior miscarriage
- Postpartum depression
- Assault
- Torture

PROLOGUE

There is a world beneath what we see. Those with their mundane lives, struggling with their rentals, their day jobs. *So much greed.* Their vehicles, traveling from state to state with indulgent freedoms.

Freedoms not gifted to others who have been locked away from society for their views on the world. Freedoms stripped away, or ended permanently.

Such spoiled lives. The boons of those who know nothing of fear.

All that is given can be taken away, just as it was ripped from my brother.

He was followed. Stalked. His purpose twisted and turned into a monstrous narrative.

His life ended on the whim of a man who

thought he understood justice when he knew *nothing*.

I grieved, for a time. Hid beneath my own blanket of fear.

That was then. Now is the time to return to the place where my brother lost his path. The path we were set on so long ago. That is what I grieve for, the man who I used to know.

The one I buried, I barely recognized.

But I know his killer.

I know where he will be.

We were the unseen, the silence that lingers in the dark to escape the light.

Waiting.

And now, I will return to complete the work that my brother failed at.

I will bring them fear, and I will illuminate their fallacy of privilege.

I will ruin their season of hope.

Simon Haldon did not die in vain.

CHAPTER 1
ARCHER

R ed Hart Ranch wasn't even in sight and yet my last trip across the country haunted me. Icy wind blasted my face despite the heating in my truck's attempt to do its job and warm the inside of the cabin.

The mountainous regions of Montana came up fast after so long in the seat. My ass was numb, but every other part of me ached for the woman I hadn't seen far in too long.

She traveled all the way to Texas for me in the meantime, for fuck's sake, then drove all the way home—without me.

Because, work.

A problem I fixed when I handed the Texas Ranger's office in Austin over into Andy Matthews' more than capable hands. The younger Ranger

3

might not have confidence in himself, but I had plenty, and now, so did his team.

Still, the thought that I should have been in Montana for the past months niggled at me over again. Where I knew I should have been since the day Simon Haldon left a mark on all our lives. Some, more than others.

The thought of the scars that Eve bore because I couldn't pull my head out of my ass a second time to see the threat right in front of me still stung.

Damnit, I left this too late.

Chasing down the man who haunted us both, tying up loose ends. That's what I spent the last eighteen months doing, until the day he turned up on my doorstep. That little venture didn't work out so well for Haldon, but the man's ghost still seemed to jinx us both. From the meagre contact I'd had with Eve, she sounded spooked every time I spoke to her, right up until the minute I left.

And then karma—spelled with a 'c' not a 'k'— hit me in full force as I realized what holiday traffic felt like all over again.

Once, I chased a murderer across state lines, following him from Texas to Montana, where I ended up at Red Hart Ranch the first time and met Eve. This time, I sought absolution and the sort of happily ever after that didn't seem realistic to a man with as many sins chalks in his column as the man I killed in the name of protecting the woman I loved.

Hence, the two day drive had become four in a solitary journey of utter silly season purgatory between never ending road works, Christmas traffic, and my own exhaustion.

Until I left Texas I hadn't realized how thin I'd left myself on energy, and spent the hours stuck in traffic battling exhaustion. Pulling in for the first night after just a few hundred miles had been more than frustrating, but it was pointless to continue pushing myself when I'd only end up as another blockage on the side of the highway.

Another statistic lost in the multitudes of holiday traffic hell. Especially when it seemed that half of the US appeared to be migrating north for Christmas.

Disappointing Eve had been the hardest part.

My phone vibrated in its holder beside the steering wheel. I flicked my gaze from the road to the screen, which lit up with my little hellion's name.

My hellion, because she had been raising hell for the past three days while I tried to make it across the country to her.

I'd left to chase my own demons across the country, and gotten stuck in my job down south, ensuring the man who had damaged her would never be free, when her grief had hit her hardest.

When she needed me most.

At least, that's what I assumed at first. Now, I wasn't so sure. The old cop in me refused to quit, but those were the sorts of questions that could wait until I knocked on Red Hart's double doors, and had my girl in my arms for the first time in months.

She'd had to rely on others for comfort while I worried that the woman at the top end of the country had grown tired of waiting for me, or had decided she needed a man closer to home.

Shoving the doubts aside that festered on regardless, I read her message. Another flashed beneath it, and I let out a laugh.

> EVE:Tell me you're at least in the right state.
>
> EVE:Don't make me come down to Texas and haul your Ranger butt back here.

Shaking my head, I shot off a quick reply, knowing she likely would jump in that white F250 of hers and drag me back home to her. Damn cavewoman. Those doubts should have stayed with my packed up house back in Texas.

I typed with my eyes half on the road, trailing

behind an infinite line of traffic that thinned the further north I drove. Thumb fumbling words and swearing at typos I used would have killed on sight, I sent back my location. A second later, my phone buzzed again.

"Eve?" I picked it up, the steering wheel jerking in my hands as I destroyed already totaled roadkill. "Dammit." That was going to stink later on when it defrosted.

"Rhys Archer. Is that how you usually answer the phone?" Eve laughed at me, though a tiny tremor at the end of her words left my gut clenching.

Fighting back the urge to floor the gas pedal, I forced a grin and managed to avoid the next road bump that used to be an animal several vehicles back. "Nah, just trying not to run over the locals."

"You're messaging *and* driving?" Eve squawked through the line. Static filled the cab of my truck as she swore liberally on the other end. *That's my girl.* "What sort of cop are you?"

I pressed my lips together, debating how to best answer her, but regardless of what I wanted to say, there was only one real answer. "The Texas Ranger sort, honey."

Eve was silent for a long moment. I glanced away from the road, but the line was still connected.

"I'm glad you're coming back, Archer. It's... It's been a while."

"Eve, I've been trying to get back since the day I left Red Hart. Hell, even you made the trip down to me. I just wanted to get back to you." I hadn't even made it to her drive and I was on the verge of begging. "But the job was there, and I couldn't just walk away."

Lies. All lies. Because I had, anyway. Walked away from her, chased a murderer across the country, then took a full year to fight my way back.

"Work." Eve said the single word like it was both a prayer and a curse.

"Always. Do you ever stop?" I asked lightly. "How's everything going in the lead up to Christmas?"

Red Hart was infamous in the local town some two and half southeast for their holiday hospitality. The memories we made last time we were together at the ranch left my heart aching for the warmth of the big house and the feel of her in my arms.

"Winding down, as always. I still miss Dad." If there hadn't been tears in her voice, there were now. I cursed myself for being so blasé.

So much happened during the year. I missed most of the fallout I caused in the wake of chasing Haldon south in my own vengeance path. Eve bore the brunt of that and survived. But...not everyone did.

"I know, honey. I'll be there soon. Tomorrow morning, if the weather holds. I keep thinking it's just hours on the road, but there's so much damn traffic. I should have come earlier."

"You should've," Eve agreed in a thick voice, and I knew she was crying. "I've missed you."

"I've missed you too, honey. It's been so long that you'll have to show me around again." The joke meant to soothe her fell flat. Her end of the line stayed silent. "Eve?"

She coughed, or maybe choked. "Some things are different around the ranch, Archer. It's not quite the same as before. Red Hart's changed. I've changed."

My stomach plummeted. *Fucking hell.* I should have trusted my gut. I *knew* she wasn't okay when she left my place the last time, and the weeks we promised each other turned into months as I recruited the three remaining officers left to complete the Ranger team in my wake. An attempt to set up Andy for success, I'd promised myself. Now I wasn't sure it had been a last ditch effort at control, or worse yet, ego.

"Are you okay, Eve?" My voice strained through a shitty line that seemed intent on hampering my voice in a wave of static or dropping out all together. "I'll push through, maybe get there around two, a bit after midday."

Dammit all. I should've walked away earlier and hauled ass to my girl like I promised.

If she still *was* my girl.

"Don't be silly." The smile in Eve's voice was contagious. Whether it was fake or not I'd find out when I arrived. Then there'd be hell to pay in one direction or the other. "Get here when you can. Don't be an accident we hear about instead."

I swallowed every misgiving and forced my own happiness through a sieve of holiday bullshit. *The games we play.* "Alright, honey. Do you need me to get anything in town on the way through?"

"If you're coming through White Cap, can you stop at Beanies? The coffee shop. I'm not sure if you remember it," she said hesitantly.

It was where I had met her. Nothing in this world could make me forget that. "I remember."

"Oh, good. I'll put an order in with Suzy, if you'll pick it up for me? There might be mail. I—" She cleared her throat. "I haven't been in for a while."

I frowned, my mouth opening to ask *why don't you send one of the boys*, but that was a tomorrow problem I'd face when I arrived. "Will do. I'll stop and collect it for you tomorrow, Eve."

I'll get to you tomorrow.

"Okay." She paused. "Archer, I'm— Just, be safe. Please?"

My heart lodged in my throat, I stared through the windscreen at the taillights of the car wavering in front of me. "Take care, Eve, until I'm there with you."

"Bye, Archer."

I blinked at the road, zoned out long after she hung up. There was so much that she hadn't said. My mind flew through different options.

Losing Len, her dad, that been hard, and that was at Christmas, too. Then she'd lost her mom, soon after. Eve went through plenty of change. Then a few months ago, when she came to me... I gritted my teeth. She'd held out at first, keeping the secrets we promised each other that we never would when I left Red Hart the first time, not ever again. When she stayed at my house she'd both opened up and crumbled all at once. Grief hit us as she told me about the baby she'd lost—our baby, and the grief she'd kept from me, and almost everyone else, maintaining a happy face.

Because that was what Eve was best at.

She made everyone around her happy at the cost of her own happiness. Something I suspected she'd done her entire life. And I'd let her do that not once, but twice.

My palm slapped the steering wheel as I cursed. I wanted to believe that she would have told me if she had been struggling with the ranch, but no. With Eve Beaumont, the chances of her fessing up to another secret, another *failure* as she would see it, were less than zero. I held back a laugh; Eve hadn't accepted help, not even when she'd needed it.

And now, I wasn't there when she did.

Cursing myself as an idiot, my mind ran through the remaining options, and halted.

Hell, had she been pregnant again, and not told me? Surely her twin brother Travis would have called me.

Fixing my focus on the road in front of me, I pressed my foot down, overtaking the car in front as soon as I had space.

And the next.

The lines between the lanes blurred as the moon rose overhead, a ghost behind a blanket of snow laden clouds. The drive north had been a dry run so far, but the weather had only held out in my favor until I hit the bottom of the mountain range.

I switched the heat up, and swore ice was formed at the corners of my windshield, though that could have been my eyes. Shaking my head, I stared at the lights that announced a small town—little more than a truck stop with a hotel at the back of it. A row of rooms for rent lined the back. As much as it would probably be a shitty night's rest in a dingy room, it was still better than sleeping in my truck in potential snow conditions.

A few vehicles were lined up for the pump. I pulled in, swiping a hand across my eyes. Pushing through to Red Hart tonight had never been a solid plan, especially if Eve needed me to pick up supplies on the way past town tomorrow.

White Cap was two and a bit hours from Red Hart Ranch. If I got some sleep now and didn't screw around in town I could be there just after lunch as I promised her earlier.

The pump freed up. I filled my thirsty truck—or maybe I'd been too heavy on the gas—and headed into the store to pay and organize a room for the night.

My stomach rumbled.

Even a Ranger had needs he couldn't ignore. And Eve... Seeing her again was a whole new level of desire. The ghost of her silken chestnut curls itched my palms. I pressed them to my thighs at the memory, a stupid grin spreading over my face.

I stopped behind a man dressed in black, lost in my fantasy of the woman I loved spread naked on my bed, until he turned around. My grin soured and slid from my face.

Eve's creepy as fuck neighbor stared at me with dislike.

The feeling's mutual, Black Hill boy.

We hadn't gotten along well the last time I'd been at Red Hart, though it was for a very different reason than I travelled for now.

The tall cowboy had a habit of wearing black and loitering around his father's ranch. Red Hart and Black Hill shared miles of boundary line that often seemed to have issues with stock staying on their own side of the fence, and the rancher's son was habitually involved. Plus, I hadn't liked the way he affected Eve.

"Pierce." I nodded, fixing my gaze at a point between his eyes.

"Archer." A slow smile stretched his thin lips.

If he'd been in Texas, I would have arrested him for breathing.

"Good to be back in Montana."

"Is it?" He watched me idly. A rich man's perk, perhaps. "Are you staying long?" Pierce half turned away, throwing his angular face into sharp relief beneath the flickering fluorescent lights.

"Long enough to become a fixture." I slipped my hand into my pocket before I punched him for no reason. Pierce had always rang alarm bells for me, and those little tinklers had saved my life fuck knew how many times.

"Enjoy your stay. You might find some things have changed up on the mountain." Pierce paid the cashier, tipping his black hat. "Have a safe drive back."

My stomach clenched. Hadn't Eve said the same thing earlier about change? It wasn't a concept I liked, but I'd tackle whatever she needed right now. More than anything, I wanted to get up to Red Hart, hold Eve and make sure she was alright. First, look after her and tackled whatever in the hell was wrong at the ranch and with my girl, I needed sleep. Driving in the middle of the night while I was pissed at her neighbor and distracted by Pierce wouldn't do either myself or her any favors.

"Sir?" the cashier called, his gaze darting

between me and the doors that swung shut behind the lanky cowboy.

I paid the man, sorting accommodation and a meal to take back to my room. Company didn't suit me right now. Swallowing the bitter aftertaste that lingered in my mouth, I headed back to my truck with instructions of where to park for the night.

As I neared my truck, my teeth began to grind. A long stripe that shouldn't have been there was carved into the perfect red paintwork, reaching as deep as bare metal. The edges of the mark were irregular, just like the tip of a key had been dug deep and ripped right along the side of my truck, higher than usual for a good key job too.

But perfect for waist height of a tall man.

I clenched my teeth harder, an instant headache blooming at my temples.

Fucking Black Hill boy.

It looked like I wasn't going to get a lot of sleep tonight, after all.

CHAPTER 2
ARCHER

The lumpy truck stop motel bed did little for my cramped back from sitting in my truck for the last three days, and nothing to ease my sleepless night when the neighboring room housed either a newlywed couple, or a brothel by the hour.

There were just some sounds that I'd never be able to strike from my mind.

I pushed myself upright before the sun crested the horizon through a thin smattering of clouds, my joints popping as I planned out the remaining miles for the day. Four hours should take me to White Cap, then two to three hours after that to reach Red Hart, depending on how well the unsealed roads behaved.

Anything to get me to Eve.

Hell, the thought of seeing her again sent a zing to my groin. I hardened instantly. Months without her... It may as well have been a lifetime of purgatory. And if I was finally getting to see the woman I had craved for so long, then a shower was the first order of the day.

Tepid water traced patterns on my back as I fisted my cock, recalling the feel of Eve pressed against me the last time I held her in Texas. How she'd knelt for me, engulfed my cock in her hot little mouth. My groan filled the bathroom that refused to steam as I leaned one hand on the cold tiles, willing myself to make the fantasy to last, but as always the thought of her brought me straight to the edge. I gripped myself tighter, forcing my orgasm back and flipped the visual to the one night we'd had at Red Hart, back in the cabin she'd given me there. Well away from the big house, we'd taken our time together. She'd knelt for me then, too, her hands gripping the bed head as I lined up behind her and sank into her heat.

Eve's instant submission, never letting go of that bedrail even as I fucked her, pulling orgasm after orgasm from her body as she shattered for me, had been the most stunning experience of my life. I'd fallen for her hard then, hell, before that even. But feeling her push contract around my cock as she gushed for me, was too much. I spilled my seed inside her as she tipped her head back onto my shoulder and collapsed for me into my arms.

The fantasy splintered as my reality caught up with me. I came on my hand with a roar, the cold room and tepid water run cool my only companion as the memory of her warm, clenching pussy faded. I hissed through my pleasure, washed away by the poor water flow as I came back to the rented bathroom with only myself and a year old memory in it.

By the time I walked out of the room clutching a fresh travel mug of burnt, instant coffee, the sun had set fire to the sky in a blaze of gold. Mercifully, the parking lot outside the motel rooms was empty. *No Black Hill Boy in sight.* I handed back my key, glad to get on the road, though I couldn't help but stare at the damage done to my truck the night before. The old animosity festered, too many bad memories replacing good ones of my time with Eve last time I was in Montana.

Forcing the thoughts aside, I concentrated on the job at hand. If I let myself slip now, I'd never reach her. Light snowfall had covered the blacktop overnight. I contemplated snow chains as a thought niggled somewhere at the back of my mind. Foregoing them after judging the amount of slush on the roadside edging to the middle, I started my truck and turned onto the blessedly empty road, though I knew traffic would increase as the day wore on.

Jason Aldean's *Got What I Got* filled the cab of my truck as I hit the cruise control, leaning back in the seat that fit me to perfection. My mind shifted back to my earlier thoughts, without the bitter tang to them.

Everything had always come back to Eve for me. For the last year while I tied up the ends of my mentor, Sam Bernie's murder. But my time hadn't just been consumed with closing up that case. I'd also set up the unit I'd headed to run more autonomously, though I knew Ethan had his head in the right space to support Andy. For a time I'd thought he would succeed me, had planned on it. But the same man who haunted Eve had ruined more than one life, my deputy and best friend high on the list. Ethan returned to duty but not in the active line of fire, preferring to drive a desk from now on.

I tapped my fingers on the steering wheel as the song ended and flicked over to something else I didn't recognize. Eve had seemed so happy—her usual self—when I initially spoke to her, but her mood slipped so fast that I wondered if she hadn't been covering up for far more than I thought. Running the ranch had always been in her. She loved the land she inherited with her twin, Travis, that had been in their family for generations, and she took a solid degree of personal pride in bettering the property, the brand, and the people who worked there.

And Christmas at Eve's table was always a treat.

That woman could cook to feed a table of ravenous men akin to an army while also giving the ranch hands she hired a home that was so much more than simply a place to hang their hat. Most of them adored her, though some did a little more than that. My mouth turned down at the thought of her body bruised and scarred at the hands of a madman I'd dispatched back to Texas.

Maybe he had left his mark too well on my girl.

The image of Red Hart's Christmas filled big house dissipated with the tainted memory. Hell, maybe Peirce was right and I was chasing a dream. I turned up the radio with clenched teeth, immersing myself in music and the countryside that ranged from gold-tipped grazing lands to snow covered pine forests that stretched over endless mountains.

White Cap came up faster than I expected, though when I checked my watch. My distraction was complete. The timing was right; I'd zoned out over the last few hours, immersed in the memory of

Eve, my fantasy of this morning. My fears of what I'd find when I turned up at her door.

If she'd want me there at all.

Nice moves, Archer. You get the girl back in just a few hours.

I was well out of practice in flirting, too straight down the line of most women. Eve, however, never objected to my style. My heart slammed painfully into my chest as I got out of my truck, tipping my hat to a pair of older ladies laden with Christmas shopping.

White Cap looked just the way it had the last time I had seen it. A tidy row of shops lined the street either side leading to the mountain habitually capped with snow year round that framed the small town with a general population of three thousand. That swelled during the holiday season, and that today, the micro floating tourist migratory population was out in force.

Parking was at a premium, but I managed to score a spot just outside the coffee shop that Eve favored for her Christmas goods. I pushed the door to Beanie's open and was hit with a heady combination of coffee and gingerbread spices. Apparently, White Cap's premium—and only—coffee shop had taken its service up a level.

Combined with the heat Suzy must have been

pumping into the place and the general lack of oxygen from the amount of people stuffed into the popular shop, my head had begun to spin by the time I made it to the first table.

I searched the heads for her grey streaks, locating Eve's best friend at the cash register. A mile long line stood out in front of her. While I figured out the best approach without screaming over the chatter that bounced off the walls in a cacophony of conversation, Suzy did the job for me.

The shop owner handed her customer over to the barista next to her and slipped out from behind the counter, her arms already raised for a hug.

"Archer! Eve called to say you'd be in. Don't you look fine?" Suzy stepped back, patting at my jacket I'd made the mistake of wearing into the shop, expecting the inside of Beanies to be as cool as the street. "You must be roasting in that thing. Now. I need to feed you before you head off. Strict instructions from the lady herself, but I won't let you leave without food enough to feed the ranch, and you know it." She fixed me with a stern eye, as though I offered to put up a fight.

"It's good to be back, Ma'am."

I tucked my hat beneath my arm, running a hand through my dark red hair. A few silver streaks worked their way through the colored ones.

Though I wasn't by any means vain about it, the fact that Eve was a good ten years younger than me slammed me once again. Sweat prickled my back, but I hadn't planned on staying at Beanie's for too long, anxious as I was to get back on the road.

Suzy hummed as she loaded her arms with goods, yelling orders to the ether.

I took the opportunity to look around, spotting a collection of carved gems and hand painted local arts on the back shelves. "You've expanded since I was here last."

"That I have." Suzy wound her way between patrons, yanking a stool out from beneath a bench that bordered on a brand new planked wooden bar. "And it's brought in plenty more customers."

"Half the town must be here," I agreed, nodding to the lunch combo she rattled off.

I planted myself at the bar, gratefully taking the craft beer that had obviously been preordained.

Bless Eve and Suzy.

Seeing Beanie's growth from the last time I'd been in town was a joy, like watching any small business owner flourish. The older woman took pride in her accomplishment, though by the looks of it, half of White Cap likely considered her family. She was certainly a permanent fixture in the town.

"Mind if I join you?" The stool beside me scraped on the cement floor.

I winced, gesturing with my beer. The place was crowded from corner to corner. "Be my guest."

A dark haired man leaned against the bar for a long moment, calling out his order to the bar staff who waved at him. A well cut leather jacket sat across his shoulders. "Joe Brunel." He settled on his stool, reaching across to shake my hand with one hand and held his whiskey in the other.

I waited for him to say more, but apparently that was all he was going to say.

"Rhys Archer." I gripped his hand firmly, and received the same back.

Dark eyes surveyed me with a hint of humor as he released my hand. "I know."

"I don't recall the name." A Ranger doesn't forget, especially not this one.

Brunel nodded, taking a sip of his whiskey and winced. "That's enough." He placed the glass back on the bar. "Yes, and no. I heard you were coming back. I'm doing some work on the land your lady owns. I'm sure I'll see more of you."

"I hope she tells good stories." I sipped my beer, though all I wanted was to get back in my truck.

"I'd say only the best, but we don't really talk much." Joe grinned, holding my gaze.

What the hell has happened to this place that all the assholes have rolled into town with Christmas cheer?

It was the inciting question I knew he wanted me to ask, but I wasn't ready to bite.

Food slid across the counter to me, Suzy beaming on the other side. I stared down at the plate cluttered with food. A steak sat between a pile of onion rings and two small rolls stuffed with coleslaw. Despite my need to get up to Red Hart, the sight of the food alone reminded me yet again that I needed to eat.

"This looks amazing, Suzy," I said as she came around to my side of the bar. I surprised her with a kiss on the cheek and ignored Joe completely. "Thank you. Now I've got questions of my own for you."

"Oh, you do, do you?" she asked, a flush rising in her cheeks. "Well, you be all Mister Texas Ranger on me and do your interrogation thing."

I held back a wince with a carefully blank face at the mention of my job, checking over my shoulder, but Joe's bar stool stood empty.

Maybe it had been a mistake to ignore the man after all. Inhaling a sharp breath through my nose, I turned back to Suzy. "I remember the story Eve told me about how this place got named wrong. *Beanies* instead of *Bernie's*. I used to work with a Bernie.

Sam. He wouldn't happen to be a relation now, would he?"

Suzy mulled it over, tapping her fingers on the bar. "Not that I can think of. Have you got a photo? There's a hell of a lot of Bernies about. Can't think of any I know down your way, though."

I scrolled through my photos until I found a picture of Sam, the one I had chosen for his obituary. Maybe it was a wild hope that there was someone else who remembered him the way I did, but grief does odd things to people.

My phone creaked in my grip as I passed my phone across to her. I filled the gap by hoeing into my food.

Suzy fell silent for a moment. "No. Can't say I knew him. Good looking, though. Must be family." Suzy beamed at me as she passed my phone back.

I grinned, shaking my head. "You said Eve called for some supplies, mail? I'm happy to take them back."

"She did." Suzy's smile dropped, and she closed her mouth.

I placed my cutlery on the bar. "What's going on up there, Suzy? Is my– Is she in some kind of trouble?" I corrected myself too late, but of all people I knew Suzy wouldn't judge me for the slip.

Hell, don't tell me Eve's doing any of this alone. Please tell me she's safe—

"She's—" Suzy stared, closed her mouth and blew out a breath. "It's been hard on her, losing both parents. And Travis isn't the same, despite having found his own happiness. He's not around as much, now that he and Rachel are married. They live at her place, most times I hear. Not having her twin around is wreaking havoc on her. She'll be glad of your company, to fill that spot."

"Will she?" I filled my mouth before I said anything else stupid.

"Rhys Archer. Are you doubting that lady? Cause it sure sounds like you are." Suzy's hands went to her hips and she glared at me.

I hoped it was at least half in jest.

"Not at all." I choked and took a too-big swallow of beer to wash the steak down, resembling a seagull with too much food in its beak. Suzy helpfully thumped my back. "It's me I'm doubting. Not her. I wish I had been back a lot earlier."

Suzy watched me finish my food for a long moment. Finally, she sighed. "She told you everything was fine, didn't she." Her flat tone made her words a statement, not a question. "Did that man leave his whiskey? That's my finest Yellowstone." She sniffed it experimentally.

"He didn't seem to like it," I said softly, watching her, though my mind went back to the man who had introduced himself and disappeared.

"Well, that's just peachy." Suzy huffed. "And sounds like Miss Eve needs a talking to." The thought of Suzy, who must have been in her sixties, dressing down a woman less than half her age who was one hell of a firecracker lifted my mood. Suzy rolled her eyes.

"Until last night, I thought she was doing okay. As usual, she hides it all well." I finished my steak and started on the onion rings.

"Always has done. I'll get your packages and you can take them up to the ranch. And tell her to come down and see me once in a while." Suzy dove into the throng that filled her coffee shop and disappeared before my thoughts straightened themselves out.

"How long has it been since she left Red Hart?" I called out to her back, but Suzy was long gone, disappearing between her rabid customers vying for her Christmas flavored lattes.

I ignored the feeling of being watched in the overcrowded space, and managed to finish my steak in peace.

HALF AN HOUR LATER, my truck was laden with boxes and food for the ranch. Eve's mail sat on the passenger seat. Suzy had waved me away when I tried to thank her, and she was too busy to answer any more of my questions, though I was also reasonably certain she engineered it that way.

"Merry Christmas, Ranger," the young man who had helped pack my truck nodded to me with a smile. He retreated back into Suzy's shop while I stared after him.

Apparently my name was all over the place. Small town talk had never been something that interested me, but it followed me all the same.

My phone buzzed against my thigh. Fishing it out, I watched Ethan's name flash up. I wanted to ignore my deputy, but if he was calling already, then either the boys were out drunk already or they had a problem. Either way, I couldn't not pick up. I connected the call in my truck, hoisting myself into the cab and pulled away from the curb, heading out of White Cap and up the range to Red Hart.

"Are you surviving up there? Lost any fingers or toes yet?" Ethan's familiar voice filled my truck as I left the small town behind.

"Not yet. Mountains only just really started. The drive is taking longer than I expected."

"Is that you telling me to leave you alone?" Ethan asked with a laugh.

There was still over two hours between Eve and I, and I hadn't planned on entertaining my staff.

"Probably." The single word broke off in my mouth, brittle and sharp. I sighed. "Sorry, man. It's been a long few days," I said carefully.

"Montana already getting to you? You can come back to Texas, you know. We'll take you in."

"You said something about leaving me alone." I grinned despite myself. Ethan's ability to keep a conversation light but get to the crux of a matter was one of the key reasons we worked so well together.

"We're all good here. Andy's tidying up Brodie's last case nicely. There were a few loose ends, and he reorganized everything nice and easy." Ethan repressed a snort on the other end of the line.

"It's what I like to hear." The thought of the office working smoothly in my absence gave me a pang. Christmas was a busy time for any law enforcement agency. Either there were too many small crimes and not enough staff, or a tragedy hit that wiped the hope out of everything. Which meant it was the worst time for me to walk away, too.

"We'll be fine. Nothing bad this year, boss."

"I'm not—"

"Yeah, yeah. Get to your girl. Have a great Christmas."

"Thanks, Mom." I rolled my eyes.

"Go get yourself get laid, Archer. You're a total ass when you don't have a girl."

"I've been bad for that long?" I asked, trying not to let Ethan's comment rile me.

He snorted down the line. "Fuck, Archer. You were born that way. Tell your girl to have a merry Christmas."

Ethan hung up before I could reply to his smartassery, but as my truck climbed into the mountains, I realized I was smiling.

Asshole.

CHAPTER 3
ARCHER

The scenery changed from pasture to mountainous foothills as I crested the last rise before the gates to Red Hart Ranch came up. The tightness in my chest loosened as the familiar pair of antlers wrapped around a heart with RHR stamped in the center, all in red, flooded the landscape. The effect of red-n-black over the original white background that I knew of the sign shimmered. Eve had ramped it up as always, and done both herself and the ranch proud.

I rolled down the window and let the chill wind bite at my face. The sharp tang of pine sank into my lungs, but the icy mountain air was welcome. I grinned as I opened the double gate chained together. Being back on the range released the tension that had coiled so tight around my own heart.

I'm here, Eve.

So damn close I could taste the honey-cinnamon sweetness of her.

The mailbox held a wad of junk mail that some poor sod had delivered under duress, no doubt. Who the hell came out this far was beyond me. I began to extract the mass with a grin; it always amused me that despite how remote Eve's ranch was, it still got a decent amount of crap delivered despite the *NO JUNK MAIL* sign pinned to the box. All her bigger items were left for collection in White Cap, of course. The grin became a frown as the wad grew larger, and a few official looking letters fell out.

Tugging the final stubborn envelope from the slot, I stuffed the armful of mail through my passenger window with the rest of her mail, and climbed back in, chaining the gate behind me.

On the other side of the entrance, weeds I hadn't noticed before, too engrossed in soaking in being back at Red Hart, twinned around the thick fence posts that held up Eve's RHR sign. I pressed my lips into a thin line. Whoever she paid to do upkeep was only completing half the job. Someone I'd have words with in short order on her behalf.

I swung up into my truck, already preparing to

rip the first worker I came across a new asshole. As I wound my way along the unpaved road through the lower portion of the property heading toward the house, I couldn't enjoy the beauty of Red Hart that had dropped my jaw on my first time up the drive with Eve. She'd smiled softly, had let me flirt with her as I soaked in the magnificence of the ranch house surrounded by two hundred thousand acres of prime grazing land that led into the forest foothills and the mountains beyond.

This time, all I saw were fence lines in desperate need of repair, derelict pump housing and a drive that badly needed grading.

I stopped looking at that point, but my brain added to a never ending list that refused to stop ticking over the closer I drove to the main house. Everything was at odds to the brand new signage that welcomed me onto the land.

Or maybe I just hadn't been as invested in the place the last time I was here. That last was an outright lie. I'd spent weeks sorting fence lines with Eve, and locating the parts of her herd that had wandered off.

I should have come back to her earlier.

Another thought I couldn't prevent floating through my mind.

I pulled into the yard in front of the ranch house.

Not another soul was in sight. The usually manic energy of the house yard lay silent, the dust settled and hard, as though no one had stepped foot outside the big house in weeks.

Maybe they haven't.

I half expected a tumbleweed to roll its way across the unsettling vista to complete the image, and was grateful when the only movement was a long doe who rubbed her neck against the fence railing and looked to me for attention.

Where the fuck is everyone?

The only vehicle parked there was Eve's white F250, tucked neatly away beside the barn. Pitiful weeds wound their way through the mags, curling around the tires. Even the rest of the stock appeared to have deserted the place. The ranch house, at least, appeared to be unscathed. The place should have been booming. Sure Christmas was the off season, everyone up here knew that. But I also knew that Christmas was Eve's favorite time of year. She made this place special on any day of the week, but come Christmas? There was no other place in the world to be right now.

On any other year, maybe.

So what in all the hells had happened to Red Hart that it looked both as stunning as it always had, but dilapidated behind its fences?

I parked beside the barn by habit, leaving room for anyone else's vehicle before it occurred to me that there wasn't *anyone else.*

Eve appeared to be entirely alone on the property.

My teeth creaked in my jaw before I relaxed the muscle or chipped anything.

Sure, her isolation would explain the state of the place, but why? Suzy mentioned her twin was off living with his new wife, Rachel. But that was one man. The ranch existed on the backs of dozens of ranch hands. A foreman who had my greatest respect. *Had.* Plenty of others. I poked my head inside the barn, calling out, but the only thing I scared off was a small flurry of chickens and a handful of spiders dangling from the crossbeam.

I tapped the door experimentally; the last time I had been at Red Hart, the whole thing had come down, injuring her brother.

Travis's name was on my lips before I drew back the shout. I raked my knuckles through my hair, considering. The next name on my list was Jude, the foreman who had become a solid friend in my weeks on the land. Hell, at this point I'd even take young Will Kirk, one of the regular farm hands who, even at Christmas, had congregated in the yard in the afternoons in the hope of being fed.

I sniffed the air, but all that hit my nose was the stale scent of animals. Even in the cold air the scent was all pervasive. The ground slushy underfoot, I strode across the yard, trying to ignore the painful clenching in my gut.

Bounding onto the veranda, I tried the door.

"Eve?" The handle gave easily, but then, she had never locked it, as far as I could tell. One of the advantages of living so far out—but also one of the deficits, especially when there was no one else around to see it all crumble.

I wondered at how much Suzy might have guessed.

I strode through the large, open plan living room, noting the significant lack of garlands and freshly cut Christmas Tree from the previous season that I remembered. Not even a fairy light winked at me. Alongside gingerbread coffees that I had a love/hate relationship with, I knew they were Eve's weakness.

"Evie?" I yelled up the stairs, the tightness growing in my chest with every step.

I should have checked here first.

Fuck, please let her be okay. Please, fucking God, please.

It'd been a long time since I prayed, and I

doubted he had anything to say to me, but right now I'd take any help on offer.

The oven was cold under my hand. For any midafternoon just a week out from Christmas, I knew just how wrong that made the situation. The confirmation hit me as a sucker punch in the solar plexus as my steps quickened. I hadn't taken off my boots, but I no longer cared about house rules.

"EVE!" I hollered again, my voice straining at the end of her name, knowing it was no use.

The enormous ranch house was empty.

I dialed her number anyway, cursing when her phone buzzed uselessly beside the coffee machine. Cute that it had charge, so at least she'd been about recently.

Clenching my teeth, I hit the front door at a fast pace, taking the stairs to the veranda at a run.

The only thing that stopped me from sprinting to my truck was a similar one to Eve's pulling into the yard. I wondered for a second if Travis had finally upgraded his beater of a vehicle to something newer, until I spotted the decals. *Wiseman & Co.* branding was plastered down its glossy white side. The truck looked as though it had never been off the black top, until now.

I halted at the bottom of the stairs, folding my arms across my chest. I didn't recognize the name, but not having been around the ranch for so long, that didn't really mean much.

A broad set of shoulders appeared in a blue, branded shirt from the driver's side. My own tensed in response. A dark hat pressed to his head as he turned, but the face that I read beneath the dark brim was nothing like the one I expected.

"Jude!" I shouted, striding to the stocky foreman, relieved to find a familiar face at last.

And maybe some answers in the middle of this clusterfuck I'd walked into.

I pulled him into a hug, which was no small thing for the barrel chested introvert.

"Archer." Jude's weathered face split into a grin. "I wasn't expecting to see you! Eve's been whining on about when you were going to come up. You took your damn time." His words were soft and packed with the emotion that fueled them.

"Has she?" I raised my eyebrows. Eve and I had been planning this trip down to the finest details— details which were swept away in the face of holiday traffic—for the better part of three months, and now I was here, I wondered how much of that planning had been one sided, or a facade. "I just pulled in. The house is empty. Do you have any idea where she is?"

Jude's gaze settled on my face while I tried to keep it smooth of the inner turmoil that consumed me. I pressed the heels of my boots into the slush beneath me, willing myself to remain still beneath his assessment.

If there was a single person I trusted at Red Hart above Eve, it was Jude. The foreman was more of a brother to her than anything else, and he had even less a propensity for bullshit than Eve did. The Ranger in me appreciated that. If it had been Travis who had pulled up, I might have had different reservations. Her twin, despite his age, was as flighty as a flight attendant on her first job.

Jude ignored my question, gesturing to someone in the cab I hadn't spotted, engrossed in the mirage of the man who had tortured Eve.

A small, chocolate haired woman climbed down from the truck. I blinked at the mirror image and shook my head. *Not Eve.* A bright smile lit her face as she approached me, dark eyes surrounded by heavy lashes sparkling in the afternoon light. Dressed in blue jeans that fit just right and a striped, red and white button down shirt, she did a better job of resembling the woman I'd driven fifteen hundred miles to find than her brother did.

"Hi. I'm Natalie." She stretched out a small hand, shaking mine firmly. Her hair was a little straighter than Eve's, curling only at the bottom, not the full head of glossy chestnut waves that made my hands itch to run through it.

My gaze slid to Jude. I'd long wondered at the foreman's attachment to Eve. Looking at the woman he had chosen for himself solidified that concept.

"Nice to meet you."

Jude slid an arm around Natalie's waist, tugging her into his side. His attachment to her was obvious in the glow between them. "Nat and I met when Travis sent me down to the auctions a while back. She's been helping us stock the ranch. Had a bit of a rocky start but," —he grinned down at Natalie who tipped her head back, her smile softening— "it's alright now."

I swallowed hard and looked away. "This place looks pretty bare."

Understatement.

Jude's gaze returned to me, forcing my attention back to the conversation we needed to have. "It is. Travis—well. He hasn't been the same since the accident."

I nodded, remembering the day he fell off the barn, who set all that in motion. "Simon Haldon changed lives."

Jude's face set into harder lines. "He did. But Trav's got Rachel now. He comes down sometimes, works with her at the vet surgery. Here, it's mostly just Eve, and me when I'm not at Nat's."

"You're still around?" I asked with a measure of surprise. From the looks of Jude, he had moved on.

"He's still here, and he still sleeps in the bunkhouse," Natalie piped in grumpily, though the corners of her mouth curved up. "Though I'm just on the other side of the ridge." She pointed to the white capped peak that loomed behind Red Hart's ranch house, pensive and stoic.

I stared up at the solitary mountain. The range spread out behind it, but that one mountain watched over the house buried at its foothills.

"That's a pretty long drive around, though. Not like there's a road straight through the middle between here and Canada." Jude grinned, rolling his eyes for my benefit. "Customs gets used to us."

"They do." Natalie snuggled into him.

"There used to be something through the range," I murmured. "Eve mentioned it once. Long time ago."

Jude frowned. "If you feel like going for a hike, ask Walker Roan. He's out on the other side of the ridge, about a day and a bit of a hike that way." He waved a hand toward the northeastern boundary corner. "He bought land from Len a decade ago. Long way back. He's not too friendly, doesn't like to talk. Trav and I went up there, helped him build the house he's got. If you want to trek in a few days further, Bode Hunter's out there too, but he'll shoot you before he talks to you. Carves the sapphires we pull out of the river. Trader Kyle talks to him." Jude scratched his chin. "Well. Kyle talks. Dunno if Bode actually talks back at all. Anyway they might know about a pass through, but no one else is out there."

"That you know about." Natalie poked him.

Jude maintained a straight face and looked at me. "That you know about," he conceded.

I watched them, my lips twitching. "That's good to know."

"What do you do?" I asked Natalie, struggling to follow the conversation.

"Elk." They both answered me together. Natalie spurred off into a fit of giggles as Jude tucked her into his chest and ruffled her hair. A stupid grin decorated his face.

The kind of stupid I kinda still wanted on my face when I finally got to see Eve.

I cleared my throat, needing to find my girl. Too much standing around after driving so far left me aching.

"Eve mentioned that she might go looking for a deer she thought hadn't been around for a while." Jude took off his hat, revealing premature grays that speckled his hair as he answered my previous question.

We all grew a little older year by year here.

"It's been gone for days," Natalie added in as she wound her arms around his waist, squeezing tight.

I withheld a groan, tapping my hat on my leg. That *did* sound like Eve, all too well.

"Any ideas where she'd look?" I directed my question at Jude, speaking over the tiny, brown haired woman wrapped around him, and tried to ignore the pang of my heart in an empty cavity.

Jude jerked his head backward. "Western boundary land. Up near—"

"Black Hill." This time I *did* release a groan. "If I'm not back by tomorrow, send the sheriff for the body. It won't be mine." I settled my hat on my head under their combined curious gaze, and headed for my truck.

Hell, I was proud of me for managing not to run.

Eve's shade drove with me as I headed for the western boundary, a reflection of the last trip we had done along this section together. Hell, that felt like an eon ago. Maybe it had been. Here, Red Hart Ranch shared a good dozen miles of fence line on the border of Black Hill land, both adjoining the Canadian border to the far north. Beyond were rugged mountains Eve had shown me, all virtually inaccessible, though she had mentioned the land used to house an original customs outpost, long forgotten, when her family first built the ranch. That was where Jude mentioned the two mountain men lived on a few days' hike out. I doubted anyone could drive into their places, which I suspected, was exactly the way they like it.

My truck ate up the miles of winding unmaintained property tracks as I lost myself in memories of looking for livestock along the boundary with Eve on a previous trip. A string of four black pickups drove parallel to my path on the other side of the boundary line jerking me out of memory lane and back to reality. An arm raised out of the driver's side cab to hail me.

I waved back, unable to make out the driver before the trucks disappeared into the tree line. I paused for a moment, letting my truck idle, but the neighbor's land wasn't my business. The sounds of the other trucks faded, and I resumed my path that followed the fence line for a short distance before I turned slightly north and headed deeper into the forest, returning to my reminiscence.

Peirce had been involved then, too, which didn't make this trip sit any easier with me. This time, though, I was looking for a girl, which was no easy feat when she was likely, knowing Eve, nowhere near the road. That trip had been a fast one, both of us belting out the wrong lyrics to a song together. This one was slower, with the window wound all the way down, though I could barely hear anything over the drone of the engine.

I parked at a familiar bend in the dirt track. The road continued on to a round trip of the property, but to access the back corner after driving for long enough that one ass cheek turned numb, I had to walk.

Which was fine. I had no idea if I had passed Eve's destination, but I had more of a chance of finding her on foot where I could hear a whole lot better. The path before me seemed a better choice than getting lost in the foothills of the mountains that I barely remembered for no good reason.

Eve was my pine needle in the snowy haystack that was Red Hart, and she could be anywhere within a twenty square mile radius, quite literally.

I paced myself, taking longer strides but kept my breaths slow and steady as I walked. My mind refused to stop ticking over, the same way it had at the house. Why the hell wasn't Jude or Travis out looking for her if they knew she was out helping her animals? Red Hart's spotted red deer herd was infamous and Eve's pride and joy. She'd do anything for her herd, and the boys knew that. Maybe Natalie had become Jude's distraction, though he seemed to be on the property to help run it often enough. I gave her twin no excuse. As part owner of the ranch and Eve's brother, he didn't get off half as lightly in my book.

I halted beside a thick pine, my palm resting on its roughened bark. Icy water dripped on the back of my hand as I listened for the faint sound I thought I'd heard a moment before, but it didn't repeat. No, it wasn't like any of the Red Hart crew to abandon their own.

Not unless Eve had a habit of taking off for days on a regular basis.

My boots crunched over snow and slush, the insides slowly soaking. I seethed silently, my footfalls careful but heavy as I strode deeper into the cold depths of the forest. What the hell had happened to my girl that she was hiking into the snow and no one knew where she was?

Or that anyone seemed to care.

My Eve, who had always brought light and warmth to the ranch hands and people who filled Red Hart, usually because of her. Every one of them adored her—some more than others, it seemed—but I couldn't see anyone hurting her intentionally.

But then, after everything that had happened to her in the last year, I hadn't been here to help prop her up, or let her cry.

God, please, let her still be able to cry.

My guts knotted as I strode through the underbrush that thinned into pine litter and mush, pausing to listen every few steps. Something warned me against calling out for the moment. The ground was soft underfoot, the snow less melted here as it had been in the yard. Small clumps of frost still clung to the trees, glazing them in a glistening array of sparkles both beautiful and blinding in reflected light.

It might have been the small change in altitude that cleared my head, but I wondered if the yard at the front of the ranch house was getting more traffic than I had assumed.

Surely Eve had *someone* helping out around the place. She'd always been as tough as hell and blessed with determination that rolled easily into the realm of stubbornness. That was what both drove me crazy and what I loved about her most, but even Eve had to admit when she needed help.

I rounded a slab of granite that always reminded me of stone boulders thrown by mountain giants, and stumbled over the first hint that I might actually have found my needle.

A ponderosa pine was split straight down the middle of its heavy trunk, the tips of the bark blackened at its shattered ends. New growth had begun to assimilate the damage done, its survival pushing through the season, but what caught my interest was the fresh turned dirt at its base. Scuffle marks spread across the pebbly soil in a wide pattern across the bowl where the tree used to stand.

I walked around it, tracing the path of destruction to a worse-for-wear oversized holly bush. Beyond that, the trail tipped down a small incline into a small dell, in a copse of elderberry and mountain laurel and right at the very bottom, Eve was planted on her perfect behind, uncoiling a ridiculous amount of wire from around a small deer that the property was named for.

She looked up as I peered down at her, my hands clenched at my sides. Dark circles hung beneath her eyes, her curls as wild a mess as the tangled deer she cradled.

But when she saw me, some part of that exhaustion was pushed away. Color rose in her cheeks, and she managed the kind of smile that sent me scrambling down the incline to help her.

"Rhys," she whispered, her head tipping back.

And suddenly I didn't give a single fuck if she wanted me there or not. Because I'd found her, and right now, that was all that mattered.

CHAPTER 4
ARCHER

"*Christ, you're a mess.*"

That wasn't what I meant to say, but it's what fell out of my mouth anyway.

"Hi, Rhys," Eve murmured. She continued to stare up at me, unmoving, clutching her deer.

I slid the last few feet of the incline through pine needles and sludge, adding to her mess, as I arrived in the little hollow she was settled in, swearing to myself. My elevated heart rate had nothing to do with the gorgeous woman at the bottom of the dip, I swore, only the fact that I hadn't face planted right on top of her as I over-balanced and caught myself at the last minute.

"Hey yourself." I crouched beside her and

nodded to the deer. "What the hell happened here? I nearly didn't find you." It was a damned miracle and I figured she knew that. The closer I peered, the more I realized that the deer wasn't the only one stuck. The barbed wire twisted about her legs as she uncoiled the deer until both of them were wrapped up like a spiked Christmas present.

Had Eve been out on her own overnight? She'd be hellishly sick if that was the case. I couldn't see any evidence of exposure, but that didn't mean there was none.

"I went out looking for her. She hadn't come home," Eve's voice caught as she studied me. Her expression stayed closed, if a little frazzled at the edges. Which was most likely exhaustion, I reasoned. "And I didn't want to lose any—her," she finished, looking down, but not before her cinnamon dark eyes glazed with unshed tears. Her flushed cheeks took on a whole new meaning.

The Eve I knew loved her animals to the point of crazy, but even when she lost a fawn, she'd been upset, but not like this.

"Frustrated, much?" I asked, kneeling next to her in slush that seeped straight through my jeans. "You've made a real mess," I said to the doe, trying not to peek up at Eve, tracing over the twisted wires wrapped around her thin legs that connected her to

Eve. "And you must be freezing," I added to the rancher who watched me.

She shrugged when I glanced up at her, the light leaving her eyes. "I was, to start with. My butt is numb. But she's really quite a warm blanket."

"How long have you both been here?" The words fell out of my mouth. I shut it with a clack of teeth. What a pathetic greeting after all this time. I wanted to hug her, kiss her, but with Eve, jobs always came first.

Not unlike myself.

Still, I couldn't bring myself to push Eve just yet. Something in the tight line of her shoulders warned me away, though that could have been the bone-numbing exhaustion that exuded from her form, as though the doe's gentle tremble, almost invisible, passed on to my girl.

"Are you asking me if I was dumb enough to get stuck under a deer all night and risk a case of hypothermia and death out here?" Eve's perfectly arched eyebrows rose in a facade of royal indignation.

I want to know how you got this far out on your own, firecracker.

But I tucked that question away for later, once I had her safe back at the house with a fire blazing after a hot shower and wrapped in her nightclothes. When she was back in my arms. But first, the deer.

I brushed my hand down her back, gauging the thinness of her shirt. I doubted she wore anything beneath it. "I'm asking if this stubborn, sexy as hell rancher stayed with her stock last night. For comfort."

"Was that a joke?"

"Best I can make after four days on the road."

Eve studied me, her smile dimming a little. "Just this morning. I'm not stupid, Archer."

Ahh. We're back to surnames.

"All right, Miss Beaumont. Let's get your deer freed." I took the rear of the animal, studying the mess it had made of itself while Eve shuffled herself closer to its head. There were no obvious breaks, just a distressed doe trussed in wire that it must have trailed from who knew where. We could find that later. But we would see the full extent when she stood and tried to run once she broke free.

"She panicked," Eve started without my prompting. "I went too fast, made too much noise, and she freaked out. She was already tangled. I have no idea where the wire came from. I'd just checked that boundary, looking for her." She caught my eye, and I remembered checking that same fence line with her, to find Pierce on the other side, having dropped a tree straight through it.

"Weren't there bison up here?"

Eve shook her head. "We sold them. I let the fields sit for months after Dad died." Her voice caught, and she coughed into her shoulder. I held back from touching her, barely. "It's just deer, now, and some elk in another field, well away from them."

"Natalie." I remembered meeting Eve's doppel-gänger back at the yard, and Jude laughing with her about the mixed herd.

Eve looked up, her fingers paused in their untan-gling. "You met her?"

"She and Jude were at the house when I arrived." I paused, staring through her, trying to eke out the information I needed to help her fix whatever the hell had happened to her. "Eve, what's going on?"

Eve dipped her head, concentrating on her task. "I had some staffing issues."

Too fast, Eve.

Alright. I could play that game. "I know all about those."

The corner of her mouth quirked, and I wanted to lean forward and kiss it.

She flicked her head and a curtain of chestnut curls with a hint of garnet fell forward to obscure her face. "I'll be you do," Eve sighed. "Everyone went home for Christmas, and I can't get any new workers." She swiped the back of her hand across her face. Her hair pushed back as she smeared her cheek with dirt.

She would have said she looked filthy. I said she looked sexy as hell.

"That's not unusual at this time of year," I acknowledged, watching her carefully. I'd already put some of the bullshit surrounding the ranch together. I wondered if she had, or if she was too close to see it.

"No. It's not," she agreed, unwinding wire from around the deer's forelegs with a small cheer. "But not even getting a promise of help from anywhere, not for next season... Rhys, the house is so empty." The longing in her voice threatened tears.

Fuck. I was right. When I wanted to be wrong.

"It's just you?" I frowned.

Eve tilted her head back to look up at me as I pulled wire off her boots, hating how the leather sliced up, but better that than her skin. "I know that look. That's your Ranger Rhys look."

"Ranger Rhys?" I laughed, a full bellow that startled the poor deer strung out between us. I pressed a hand to its hind quarters, murmuring low and soothingly until it settled. The seasons dropped away until I remembered in full what it was like to be back on this land, the weeks I'd spent here when I first met Eve, working here shoulder to shoulder with the men who ran the land for her.

Worked alongside *her*.

"You make me sound like a park ranger off on a jaunt with Yogi Bear."

Eve smothered her yelp as I tugged too hard on a wire, flapping at me. "Well, maybe a little more than that," she conceded with a smile. Some of the sparkle returned to her eyes, and that alone made the drive across the country worth it.

I'd do anything to make this woman happy.

Anything.

I dipped my head, tugging gently at the end of the length of wire she passed over to me. My own tangle seemed endless, but finally I managed to pick it free. "A pair of wire cutters would have been handy, you know."

Eve grinned. "Yeah, I should have gotten you to find some. I— I got frazzled. Left my phone in the house. Panic hit me, and I had to get her free."

I huffed a soft laugh. One of the things that attracted me most to Eve was her ability to cut clear through the bullshit factor. That, and her strength. Both internal and external though I knew she never saw herself that way. She had come through so much, and I met her at the peak of her duress, or so I'd thought. But even the strongest only gained strength from the people supporting them.

"I've missed that." I spoke to the deer's leg, running my hands over her rump in a quietening motion.

"What?" Eve jerked her head up, staring at me.

I met her cinnamon gaze. "This place. You. How direct you are."

How fucking beautiful you are.

I caught the last words before they could escape. Now wasn't the time for romance. That could come later, if she let me. Right now I needed to fix everything that was crumbling around Eve in an effort to prop her up when everyone else turned away from her. When they *forgot* her.

I refused to let that happen for one more night.

A sardonic smile curved my lips. Ranger Rhys was back, indeed.

"I've missed you, too," Eve whispered, ducking her head. Thick lashes covered the eyes that were a window into every inch of her soul that was just Eve, something she'd given me access to before.

No matter how I tightened my grasp on her, the further she slipped away from me. And I'd only just arrived.

"Eve," I murmured, freeing the deer.

It shook itself all over us. Grit and mud splattered everything around the deer as it scampered away on four perfectly healthy, stable limbs.

I brushed my finger over a spot of mud that joined the streak already marring Eve's cheek.

"Mmhmm?" She raised an eyebrow at my wince.

"Uh, you've got —" I kept trying, but only succeeded in spreading mud about her pale, clear skin.

"You're making it worse, aren't you?" Eve laughed, peering up at me.

Even with her hair in a wild mess of chestnut curls that cascaded over her shoulders and mud smeared across her face, my heart battled for space in my chest.

"You're beautiful. And yes," I replied at her sharp inhale.

You don't have to do it all alone, Evie.

But she wouldn't appreciate me barging in, just yet.

Eve studied the ground. "Thank you for coming up."

"You don't need to be so formal with me," I murmured, sliding my hands beneath her arms to help her up as the last of the wire fell away with the deer's escape.

A loud *squelch* filled the hollow as Eve rose.

Giggles burst from her. She clutched my arms, extracting herself from the mud and taking a whole lot of goop along with her.

"How long did you say you were down there again?" I asked into her hair, attempting not to seem stalkerish as I inhaled her scent.

"A few hours," she murmured, sliding her hands around my forearms and let them rest there.

"And you really didn't think to take your phone with you?" I asked, savoring her warmth.

Fuck knew why I chose that hill to die on in that moment, but I'd planted my flag with her name on it, and die for her, I would.

Her skin stood out as pale against the dark red of my shirt, and despite the cold muck seeping between us, I pulled her into me in a backward hug, wrapping my arms tight around her chest.

She sighed, leaning her head back, staring into the entwined branches above us. "Who would I call for help, Archer?"

Still Archer.

We'd have to work on that.

"Me," I said into her hair, kissing the top of her head.

"But you weren't here."

"I said I would be, today. Don't you remember?"

I turned her in my arms, inspecting her, but I saw the same Eve I remembered.

It was her eyes that held the most difference. Instead of locking in on me, they were vacant, rather like her mother's had been in the days after her father's death.

I crushed her against my chest, winding my arms around her and promising never to let her go.

Until she began to wriggle.

"Breathing." She tapped my arms.

I loosened them, fairly certain that it was her attempt at a distraction, but I gave her the benefit of the doubt, regardless.

"You can breathe," I said, pressing my lips to her forehead. "And you shouldn't be alone."

"I'm not," she said, completely reasonably in the circle of my arms, and completely at odds with her words of a moment ago.

I sighed, the pressure I had expected to ease when I finally found her building exponentially. "Let's get you back to the house. A shower and some clean clothes, alright?"

Eve nodded, letting me curl my fingers around hers and lead her back to my truck, coiling the wire the doe had been trapped in around my other hand.

I didn't need to ask where her truck was; I knew it was parked in the yard by the big house.

"You came up here alone, did you?" I scanned the tree line as we walked; old habits and all.

Eve shot me a look over when I glanced back over my shoulder that told me she knew exactly what I was doing. "When I couldn't get workers, Pierce offered me some of his. An offer I couldn't refuse." She huffed at the irony, but her jaw was clenched tight.

"And how did that go?" Her silence said everything. "Eve?" I tugged her to a stop. For a long moment, she refused to look at me.

After an eternity, Eve raised her stunning face to me. Unshed tears danced in her eyes, a vulnerability I both hated and loved stared back at me, all strong and fierce and proud.

Hell, I loved her.

"You haven't been here, Archer," she whispered, searching my face. "You have no idea what this year has been like." Dark lashes surrounded burnt cinnamon eyes that drew me in. A bead of a tear clung to one.

Very slowly, terrified of widening the abyss between us, I lifted my hand to brush the tear away. Eve blinked at me with an innocence shadowed by something I couldn't quite identify. A breath passed between us, a fragile peace offering. My hand dropped to squeeze her shoulder, rubbing my thumb over the curve of it, and she jerked back like she'd been whipped.

She had.

I cursed myself for my stupidity as she whirled away, and was in the passenger seat of my truck before I could take five steps to follow her.

Pressing my lips together a myriad of images flooded my mind, but I pushed them all aside to focus on the breathing woman before me. I threw the wire into the bed of my truck and swung up into the cab, starting the engine as I cursed myself and the man who hurt her both.

The ride back to the ranch house was silent.

Four black pickups, all similar to the ones I'd seen trailing through Black Hill land earlier in the day were parked in the yard outside the ranch house.

Jude stood on the veranda steps, his arms folded across his barrel chest. New lines I didn't remember feathered the tanned skin around his eyes, his face shuttered as he watched us pull in.

I glanced across at Eve, my hand raised to take hers. The trip back across Red Hart was nothing like what I planned. She'd shut down on me completely, and the months we'd been apart and everything that happened between us in the last year spread thin on the ground that my tires ate until neither of us ended up saying anything at all.

I ached to hold her, kiss her, promise her everything would be alright. But I did none of those things, believing that a shower, a meal and time before the fire would give us what we needed to start again.

And again, as we pulled into the yard before the big house, I realized that I'd given her far too little far too late.

"Evie," I murmured, reaching for her, but she shot out of my truck, slamming the door behind her.

I winced, climbing out slower. Watched as she approached Jude and spoke to him quietly. And moved on.

A man dressed in a black shirt and blue jeans took off his hat as Eve approached him on the veranda, a broad grin that didn't suit him splitting his face.

A face I recognized from Beanies.

Eve trotted up to him, giving the man a hug, greeting him warmly.

"Hi, Joe."

Joe Brunel bent to return her embrace, his words warm as he stared at me over her head with a challenge lighting his gaze.

"Hi, Eve."

CHAPTER 5
ARCHER

J oe caught Eve's hand, tugging her up the steps to the ranch house. She looked over her shoulder at me with wide eyes. Something that I couldn't identify in them made me hesitate.

At the top of the veranda steps, Jude stared down at the ranch hand, his arms still folded across his broad chest. Joe said something I couldn't hear, and Jude nodded, shifting side to allow the taller man entry.

I turned away Jude started down the stairs toward me, my hand on the door to my truck by the time he reached me.

"You must need a pit stop after driving all that way," he said behind me in the quiet, reserved way I'd always associated with him. Absent Natalie, he'd reverted to the foreman's personality I remembered. If this was what I'd been greeted with when I turned up at Red Hart, I might have had less concerns.

Burt it wasn't.

The man I used to know had been then and this was... Now. What I thought I'd find in Montana looked nothing like what I remembered.

I didn't turn away from watching Eve embrace another man like they were intimate. For all I knew, they were. "Before I saddle up and head back home?" I asked Jude, not bothering to remove the bitter edge that tainted my words.

"It's not like that. She's missed you. Damnit, Archer. She's talked of nothing *but you* since you both started talking about you coming back."

"But you didn't know I was coming for Christmas. This week. She didn't say anything." *Did she?* I held my breath, but Jude's silence behind me said everything I needed to hear. But I still needed to pick a fight with someone, anyone who got in my path. "Well?" I demanded, swinging around.

Jude fixed me with a steady gaze. "You haven't been here."

I snorted. "That's what she said."

"And I know you couldn't get back, Archer. You did what you had to do. Nobody blames you for that."

A second snort.

I blamed me for it.

"And doing everything the right way—where exactly has that gotten me, Jude? She's in there with another man, for Christ's sake."

Jude lifted both eyebrows. "Then what are you doing out here?"

I opened my mouth to fight back, but something in his face stopped me. I peered closer. "Are you *smiling?*"

"Yes, sir." Jude nodded toward the house. "And I'm going to help a certain lady cook for everyone, seeing as she looked a little uh, worse for wear when she arrived." Jude paused midstride, looking at me askance. "You didn't actually—" He waggled his eyebrows. "—right away, did you?"

I stared at him with hard eyes that had made a lesser Ranger flinch. "Do you think I'd be this fucking antsy if we had?"

"Good point." Jude clapped my shoulder, steering me toward the house. "Beer?"

"Please."

Inside Red Hart's stunning ranch house seemed warmer with a host of people cluttered in her belly than it had with me running about shouting Eve's name along vacant halls. Jude poured me a beer, refusing to let me serve anyone else. I took it with as much good grace as I could, watching the men Pierce had 'lent' Eve mingle around the long table set off to one side of the open space, eating her snack food and talking too loudly.

None of that would usually bother me, but not one of them raised a hand to help in an otherwise empty house. I noted the oven was already warming with bake trays filling the space.

As soon as I made a move to help, Jude fixed me with a hard stare, but the moment his back was turned, I headed out the back door to where I knew the wood pile resided. Situated at the rear of the house, the white capped mountain that framed Red

Hart Ranch loomed over me. But rather than being dwarfed by the majesty of the behemoth, I was in awe of it.

Some primal part of me wondered what was on the other side. I recalled Natalie saying that she lived over the Canadian border, which must be a royal nuisance to Jude, getting to and from her place.

Humming *The Bear Went Over the Mountain* to myself, my lips quirked in a stupid smile that had nothing to do with the beer I had downed. I loaded my arms with the last of this year's dried firewood. Protected from the weather, it was perfect for burning now. But the rack seemed sadly depleted, and I added splitting firewood—if there was any cut —to my list.

Which was growing fast.

Jude and I needed to talk. But first, I refused to let the ranch house fall prey to Eve's somber mood. Hell, lifting it back to its usual Christmas spirit might actually help her.

"Damn. I didn't think of it," Jude muttered as he massacred elk patties on the stovetop.

"You're doing enough," I called, adding him to my list.

Warmth spread through the open plan living area in a sunset glow that appealed to the dying early evening light. I'd spent more time than I thought on the western boundary with Eve, the dapple light already low in the forest. The decent drive back stole extra hours I didn't have to give, and suddenly I craved the solitude I'd hoped for in holding her while she explained what the hell happened here.

Now I knew that wouldn't happen.

Jude continued to attempt to cook and when I joined him to assist, I noted some of Joe's friends filter into the living room, filling it with conversation and laughter.

When Eve appeared at the top of the stairs, I paused, watching her small frame, thinner than she had been the last time I had seen her, I was sure.

Still, she was the epitome of stunning as she walked slowly down the stairs, taking in the ambience I'd helped to build. She halted on the bottom step gripping the banister with clenched fingers.

I stopped chopping the vegetables that Jude hadn't kicked me out of the kitchen for stealing from him.

"Go to her," the foreman nudged me. "If nothing else, Archer, the girl needs a damn good loving. Bring her back to us."

I laid down my knife in an instant. Flashing a grin to my friend that faded just as fast, I went to meet her. Not that I needed his permission, but this was Jude's domain as much as it was hers. Maintaining the status quo had always been key at Red Hart.

"Eve." I caught her on the bottom step of the stairs, so she stood at perfect eye height with me.

She halted, her eyes cautious. I hated that we weren't on even ground straight up, but hell, if I had to work to earn her trust again, then I'd put in the hours. I smiled, risking brushing my hand across her waist where a leather tie belt cinched in her denim dress that flowed to her ankles. Buttons were done up in a neat row from her ankles to mid chest giving a tantalizing glimpse of flesh. Her damp curls dried fast in the heat as the temperatures plummeted outside. I knew it would snow tonight.

I swallowed hard as she let me touch her, the warmth of her body seeping through the scarred pads of my fingers. "This is new. I—" My throat closed up, leaving me as speechless as a schoolboy talking to his first crush.

"I missed you too." She stared at me with fathomless eyes I swore I could fall into and never emerge.

Hell, I didn't want to.

"Was I this useless to you last time I was here?" I murmured, grazing my fingers across her hip in a back and forth motion, enjoying the way her breath hitched a little too much.

Her gaze flicked up and over my shoulder. "Maybe you were better then," she acknowledged, her cheeks flaring with color. "Archer—"

"I know. Not in front of the locals." I dropped my hand and stepped back to let her pass.

Eve stepped down from the last step, and looked up at me. The color remained in her cheeks as she tipped her head back, defiance and awareness vying for dominance in her honey and burnt cinnamon gaze. "Damnit, Rhys. It's my house. I should be able to talk to a man when I want. Without worrying. But I do." What started out as a huff transformed into a worry, her brows meeting in the middle.

I ached to fold my hands around her waist and draw her into me, shielding her from the world, but we weren't there, not yet.

"When you're ready," I said in a low voice, keeping our conversation private from the rest of the room. "I'm yours, Eve. But not until you ask. Until then, I'll respect those boundaries." *Even when they sting like fuck.*

Eve swayed toward me. "Even if I want you to shatter them?"

I swallowed hard. "Ask me again at the end of

the night when everyone's left," I murmured. "See how you feel then."

Fuck me if I didn't want to take her up on that offer right here in front of everyone. But right now, what she chose mattered. If Eve changed her mind then I'd respect that choice, even if it wasn't the one that I wanted.

The faintest smile played at the corners of her mouth, tipping them upward in the sort of motion I wanted to lick. "Good," she murmured as she passed me, her hips sashaying in a way that left me clenching my teeth to hold back the urge to ignore everything we just said and kiss her in front of everyone, claim her as mine. But then she'd run, and the fragile trust we'd garnered would never settle between us.

Someone at the long table groaned, and it took everything in me not to slap the fucker on the back of the head. Thankfully Jude called dinner, and I made my way with the rest of the small crowd to the kitchen, grabbing a plate and filling it full of food.

Eve ate alone, with Jude. Neither of them sat at the main table. That was something new. More trust issues, or maybe Jude was protecting her. Either way the new process had my approval. Even though it meant that I spent less time with her, it also meant the other ranch hands kept their eyeballs to themselves.

"You staying the entire season, Archer?" Joe called from the other end of the table as I finished my steak and dived into my sides of vegetables.

The drive and digging Eve out of the mud took a hell of a lot of energy, more than I expected. I devoured my food before I bothered answering the man I'd developed a strong dislike for.

"As long as it takes." *Forever, asshole.*

"You got family up this way?" *Why are you here?*

"Only the people in this room." *Keep your hands and eyes to yourself.*

"Good to know there's a measure of trust already established. *Don't fuck with what I have.*

"I've got a history with Red Hart." I sat back and sipped the beer Jude handed me, sliding onto the long bench seat at my side to solidify my claim in silence.

The unspoken conversation Joe and I hosted died a quick death. I hoped he got what he looked for from his probing, as much as I took from his side. The silent run of messages were a two way street. Jude leaned back with his arms folded, his eyes closed as men finished up with their plates and began to disperse for the evening.

"Ten minutes, tops. Get your shit and get out.

Leave the lady of the house alone for the night," he called, his voice rasping with disuse.

"Does that include you?" Joe stopped beside us, seemingly unwilling to let the conversation drop. Someone sniggered nearby as I held his gaze and let my beer bottle rotate slowly in my hand.

"I have business with Archer." Eve appeared on my other side. The beer slipped from my hand, hers grazing mine as she took a sip. "But Jude's right. The big house is closed for the night. There's a few things I need to catch up on." Her gaze swept around the table until it landed on me. "You. Stay."

Jude's hand clapped my shoulder. He leaned in. "Good luck. I'll see if she's mauled you in the morning."

"Fuck off," I muttered back under my breath without any heat.

The rest of Joe's crew filed out of the house, their conversation raucous. I never shifted from my seat on the bench, not until the last man left the house, Jude shooing them out of the ranch's double doors. Only then did I start to rise, my plate in my hands.

"Sit," Eve ordered abruptly. "I didn't tell you to go anywhere."

I returned to my seat as she stood over me. "I thought we had a different conversation before, honey."

Her hand grazed across my shoulders before she took Jude's spot beside me, sitting with her legs tucked beneath her, facing outwards, opposite the way I did. "We did. I'm just... I'm so tired, Archer."

She turned her head to face me, some of her hair tumbling out of the messy bun she'd tied it into over dinner. I risked capturing one, winding the silky strand around my finger. Breath stalled in my chest with her so close that I couldn't take another.

"I know, honey. You want me to sleep down here so you know you're safe tonight?" It was a poor offer. I would have done it anyway, and we both knew that.

"Maybe." Her fingers twisted in her lap. I fought the urge to draw her closer. "The house is always so quiet now."

"You kicked them out," I said reasonably.

"But they aren't the company I want." She faced me in full, pulling her hair from my grip, angling one knee up on the bench. "What happened, Rhys? What changed when I wasn't looking?" Her eyes widened, searching my face for answers that I couldn't give her.

"I don't know, honey. But I promised I'd stay, and I'm not leaving you alone again, alright? I promise you, Eve," I said in a low voice. "Not even if you kick me out. I'm here."

"But I'm not the girl you can have forever with," she whispered, her pretty eyes shimmering until the burnt cinnamon color was consumed amongst a sea of shattered hazel.

I cupped a hand at her nape, massaging small circles there until her eyes closed. The tears she'd held at bay spilled over. I brushed those away carefully with the pad of my thumb. "You want to tell me something, Evie?" I murmured. "Anything at all?"

She shook her head, denying what I knew was coming. My stomach clenched, waiting on the inevitable. "I—"

But she couldn't. What wasn't said hung between us. I slid my hands around her as she stilled, letting me lift her onto my lap. I kept every movement slow and even, giving her plenty of time to push me away or tell me *no*. She never did, even when I checked in with her.

"Eve, tell me to put you down any time, alright?" I kept my massage on her nape a constant.

She shook her head. "I don't want you to stop." The tears flowed harder as I nodded, pressing butterfly light kisses to her eyelids and cradled her to me.

"I'm not gonna let you go, honey. But I want to kiss you. You can say no—" I swore my heart broke on that offer alone. "—If you want. Anything you need to say no to, you go right ahead. Alright?"

She nodded, and tipped her head back. "Please?"

The sound that ripped from my throat was feral and low. I bit it back, unwilling to scare her. My mouth touched hers, the kiss soft and sweet and brief. I pulled back after the lightest contact, but she shook her head.

"More, Rhys. Like the night in your cabin."

I breathed hard, every fantasy I'd had of this woman for the past minute coming true at once. But she seemed so fucking fragile and the thought of hurting her scared me. "Evie, I don't want to cross any boundaries with you." I nuzzled at her throat as she moaned for me, twisting on my lap, seeking my mouth.

I finally let our lips contact again, gliding my tongue across the seam of her mouth. She gasped for me, arching in my arms. I let out the groan I'd been holding back, and covered her mouth with mine, pushing my way inside. Just the thought of being close to her was intoxicating, The feel of Eve beneath my hands became my new religion. I pulled her body against mine, needing to feel her closer. The warmth of her body seeped into mine.

"Christ, I need you," I rasped into her mouth.

The tip of her tongue flicked against mine, her

soft sigh as she let me in, sending a shot of pure need straight to my cock.

Her breasts pressed into my hands, and I played with a taut nipple, plucking and pinching until she writhed in a hot mess over my legs. I flicked one button on her dress, then the next, rubbing her cheek with my chin, the rasp of my stubble enough to draw a gasp from her. I dipped my head to lick her exposed cleavage, sucking on her flesh hard enough to mark.

Eve moaned for me, holding me to her as I sucked her nipple free from the material and flicked it with my tongue. She moaned, twisting beneath my ministrations. The dress material twisted as I pulled on it and raised my head.

"Eve, let me take you upstairs. Somewhere better than this—" I gestured to the long table with its hard wooden benches.

Eve's hands on my chest, pushing back were a douse of cold water.

"Stop," she murmured, shoving backwards.

I caught her before she fell off my lap, helping her readjust her dress. "Eve," I rasped, near shaking my head to clear it. "I scared you. I'm sorry. That was too fast."

"No. I shouldn't have. I know better." She stared

up[at me still panting. "I just— I miss human contact so much. I miss *you*."

I frowned at the double negative, trying to work out what she needed most. "Last time we were together in Texas, I damn near proposed to you." I traced the bare skin at her throat. "I gave you a necklace made for you. That was my promise I'd be back. Remember?"

Her hand raised to cover my fingers. "I remember," she whispered. "I don't wear it, I'm scared it will break and that matters."

My rapid heartbeat slowed a little. "I get that, Eve. But wear it. For me, if you want. Please?" I leaned in, hesitated, and pressed a tender kiss to her lips.

Her sharp inhale left me spinning as her lips parted and she licked my bottom lip.

"Eve...fuck," I cursed, pulling her closer. "If we keep going I'll take you upstairs and we're gonna end up in your bed, honey. I can take it slow for so long but... Hell."

Eve kept exploring, running her hands along my chest, licking at my mouth. "You taste sweet."

I growled, lifting her to straddle my hips and pushed myself up to stand. "Remember what I said about your bed, honey?"

She made a soft sound in the back of her throat

that I took to mean that she didn't object to me carrying her up the stairs. I took each step carefully. One arm wrapped around her as I walked, still kissing her. Every time our lips and tongues met, our kisses grew rougher. Sure, we started slow but as every time with Eve, my control frayed.

I kissed her harder until we crashed into the door of her room—fuck, I hoped it was her room.

"Is this one yours?" I asked, breaking the kiss long enough to give her air.

"Mmhmm." She glanced about to give me confirmation, then her tongue slid back into my mouth.

I groaned, my cock pressing hard against her heat that rubbed my jeans. The denim dress she wore hiked around her hips, flowing over her bare knees. I gripped beneath her thighs, holding her tight to me as I kicked the door open and found her bed, lying her down onto it.

"Tell me to stop, Eve. If you don't, you know this changes everything."

"I need you tonight, Rhys."

I stared down at her in the darkness, light filtering in through the doorway from downstairs. "Fuck, you're so beautiful. I've thought about you every damn day," I murmured, spreading her thighs wide with my legs, settling into her heat.

SOFIA AVES

She arched for me as I worked the buttons on her dress, her hands tugging at my shirt. Desperation drew us both forward, our kisses hot and rough, open mouthed and wet licks. She shivered and panted as I ground against her.

"Fuck, beautiful. You're gonna come for me already?"

Eve mewled beneath me as I spread her dress open, baring swollen breasts and the swell of her soft tummy. I dipped my head, sucking and licking her nipples as I rubbed against her, the seam on my jeans grinding against her clit. She shivered, whimpering as heat and the scent of sex flooded her bedroom.

"Christ." I swore, releasing her nipple with a pop and slid my fingers along the dampness spreading over her panties. "That was fast, honey. Can you do that again with my fingers inside you?"

Her answering moan left me hard enough to disgrace myself. I coated my fingers in her slick and slid two inside her. Eve's pussy clenched down as I drove her to the next edge. Her cries shattered around the room, her tight body milking my hand as I worked her over.

I growled my own need, shucking my shirt off. "Lie back, honey. I'm not done yet." I knelt between

86

her legs, throwing one curved thigh over my shoulder.

Eve's hands tangled in my hair as I licked her pussy, cleaning her orgasm from her swollen flesh. The sweet scent of her permeated the room, leaving my head spinning. I swore I'd come in my jeans at the mere thought of sinking into her, but I kept my head in the game, focusing on the task before me. Her thighs clamped around my head as I lapped at her folds gently, focusing on her sensitive spots.

"Please, Rhys," she screamed, as I sucked on her clit, flicking the nub back and forth. "Please—"

I flicked her clit again, sliding a finger inside her pussy. She came hard for me, soaking her sheets.

"Such a good girl," I praised her.

Sliding in beneath her boneless body, I tossed her clothes out of the way, tucking her naked body against mine. The quilt had slid a long way down. I hooked that with my foot, pulling it over us, and pulled my shirt back on, leaving it unbuttoned as I cradled Eve to my chest.

"Archer?" she murmured, pressing her lips to my chest.

"Shh, honey. Sleep."

"Mm. Why aren't you—"

I smiled, stroking her hair gently as I tucked her into me and closed my eyes, propped up against the headboard. "Sleep, Eve. I promised you that I'm not gonna leave you. And if you want that every night, then I'll give you that."

"But I want–"

"Go to sleep, honey," I said firmly, knowing that was exactly what she wanted. If she kept asking I might not have the strength to not roll her over and fuck us both into blissful oblivion. "Take what you need from me."

"I'll tell you what I need," she grumped at me prettily.

Her breaths deepened and with the amount of orgasms her body took from me, she dropped into sleep within scant minutes. Eve curled around me, her warmth and scent the sweetness I stole a few hours' sleep rest with my arms wrapped around the woman I loved.

CHAPTER 6
ARCHER

My first mistake was that I didn't fuck Eve the night before because I knew she'd regret it today. My second was leaving her before she woke.

Fast cooling coffee didn't sear my throat half as much as I required it too as my little hellion in caramel calf boots that I'd bought her the season before sauntered down the steps of the big house and straight across the yard past me without a single flicker of recognition. I watched Eve's ass sway in those damned tight jeans I wanted to peel from her body and cursed inwardly.

Shoulda gone all the way, cowboy.

But the fact that I was a Texas Ranger on Montana soil sliced through me as she strode right up to Joe Brunel and flipped her hair over her shoulder, chatting animatedly about whatever project she'd woken with on her mind.

A project that clearly wasn't me.

A throat cleared at my side. I didn't need to look up to know Jude studied me like I was a misbehaving buck he wanted to understand better.

"I spent time with her last night, alright?" I groused finally when his pensive silence grew too thick.

A subtle cough raised my irritation levels beyond my capacity. "Not good enough, apparently. Didn't I tell you she needed a damn good loving, Archer?"

I let out a frustrated noise. "I wanted to take it slow with her, alright? Something's happened since I was last here and... Fuck it." I blew out a breath and faced him, turning my back on the sight of Eve flirting with another man. I knew she did it just to shit me—hell, I hoped that was the case. "She told me about the baby, Jude. It's broken something inside of her."

He watched me and nodded, turning back to his work. "Which one?"

My world plummeted.

The fact he didn't look at me when he said it should have been my first clue. I grabbed his shirt and yanked him back to me. "What the fuck do you mean, *which one*?" I kept my voice low, though blood pounded at my ear drums. I barely made out his answer, sound catching up halfway in.

"...I told you Will Kirk saved her life last season, when we saw him in White Cap, right?"

I nodded as he peeled my fingers from their death grip on his shirt. "Yeah, you mentioned." My voice came out hoarse, but Jude remained steady and quiet.

"He carried her out of the forest when it lit up. We had a huge fire here a few weeks back. Up in the eastern corner, on the way up to Walker Roan's, right before the storm that put it all out. We found the source..." Jude shook his head. "Anyway, Will walked out Eve in his arms, carried her through the smoke and mother fucking flames like a wraith. He nearly died, picked his ass right up again, went back in with Gage and one other for the woman he loves, and dragged her out too. He's covered in scars head to toe from it. Not quite the pretty boy he used to be." Jude ran out of air and sound from the longest speech I'd ever heard from him.

Every word was worth it, but he still hadn't said what I needed to hear.

"And Eve?"

Jude's mouth set in a tight line. "Trav and I took her back to the house, called the doc, but we couldn't—" He exhaled a slow breath. "It's why Trav stays away. He can't bear to look at the sister he couldn't help."

I stared him straight in the face. "And you?"

He met my eyes without flinching. "I'll be here to pay my penance for not being able to save the baby she lost twice over. I'm sorry, Archer."

Fuck.

I closed my eyes as my heart shattered. For her. For both of us. Again.

Jesus, she'd already been through this and to lose what she wanted, what I thought she wanted a second time, under those circumstances...

And I still hadn't been here.

Last night, I thought I made the best choice for both of us. The safest choice.

I blew out a harsh breath as Jude's hand gripped my shoulder tight, hard enough to hurt. I took the pain he offered, turned it into something useful.

"What jobs have you got for the rest of the day?" I turned the rope over in my hands that I'd been splicing.

Jude was silent for a second, then his hand dropped away. "Maybe I'm not the best person to ask that."

I raised my head, thankful my vision was clear as I looked up. Eve stood before me, her hair slung back over her shoulder, phone clutched in her hand. My lips managed to turn up at the corners at that one, though my smile died a short death at the fire that blazed in her eyes as stared back at me. Not impassive, and it was a glare, but somewhere in between.

I wanted to fall on my knees and beg her forgiveness.

I wanted to kiss the hell out of her before every man in the yard.

I wanted to take her upstairs and spank the shit out of her and—

Damnit, Jude was right. And that advice wasn't a one way street. The realization hit me far too late, but I couldn't rectify that right now.

"What can I do for you today, Miss Eve?" I risked the use of her first name, holding her gaze as I always had, daring her to meet me head on.

Last night was everything I wanted.

Falling asleep with her in my arms, exhausted and boneless and stunning. I could only pray it was enough. What she wanted too.

"I don't need you today, Archer," Eve's voice was distant, her gaze fixed at some distant point beyond me.

"You don't." My teeth clenched hard. Pity my tongue was in the way. My eyes watered.

Fucked that one up well and truly.

Over Eve's shoulder, Joe sent me a wink.

"Maybe you could work with Jude for a while," Eve murmured, drifting away. I could almost see her mind ticking over as she moved on to other things, the way she always had.

I caught her hand as she turned away. A deep flush stained her cheeks. I managed not to brush my knuckles over the spots of color or kiss her. *Just.*

"Eve—"

"Please, Archer," Eve murmured, tugging her hand from mine.

I let her go.

Jude met me out at his truck, but I shook my head, grabbing the driver's door to my own vehicle.

"I don't want to break yours."

"Fair enough." Jude made it around to the passenger's door before I threw my truck into gear and peeled out of the yard in a cloud of dust.

It was childish, but a far better option than laying Joe out cold on the hard packed dirt in front of the big house where Eve could see the venom ripping through my veins.

Maybe.

My gaze narrowed, zeroed in on that firm, round behind that I wanted to slap, or maybe bite. But it wasn't where my brain was at.

Eve needed cowboys. Real ones. I'd get them for her, with a little help.

"Jude, we're going into town."

The introverted foreman groaned, lifting pain-filled eyes to meet mine. Though he hadn't spoken, I answered him anyway.

"Yes. We do."

Jude grumbled the entire way down the drive. The man's hard work ethic was undeniable, with his loyalty still clearly to Eve and the ranch, despite her brother's obvious absence, but he hated leaving the land. He'd spent so many years on the ranch that getting back out into town nearly crippled him, though I was grateful for his company. I'd need that loyalty later in the day.

Thankfully, there was reception at the gate, and Suzy picked up faster than I expected, my snow chains barely grabbing in the light slush.

"Mister Texas Ranger! How are things up on the

mountain?" Suzy's voice blared through the speaker where it dangled on my knee, background noise providing additional static.

I gritted my teeth, and threw a cautionary look at Jude, but the foreman sat with his hands pressed to his knees, his elbows locked.

Maybe it was my driving.

"It's all good, Suzy. We're good."

"Uh huh." Skepticism filled her tone, and I bit back a laugh.

"Fine, that was bullshit. I need hands up here, and Eve needs a friend. Any chance you can come up and bring half the town to work on the ranch for the season?"

"Now you're swearing? You never cease to amaze. I can't come up, and I can't bring the town, but I'll send a truck load of boys back with you. Got a certain Mister here who can't stay on the back of a cow—uh, a bull—and would love some work. Are you just leaving Red Hart now?"

I grinned at her enthusiasm. "I'm already on the road."

Jude jerked his head in an abrupt nod.

Nope, that was my driving.

"I'll have your care package ready to ride when you get down here." Approval coated Suzy's voice. "And Archer? You'd best be looking after my girl."

"Yes, Ma'am." I hung up, shaking my head with a soft laugh.

Suzy was certainly one of a kind. But she loved Eve, and she probably knew something was up. I'd had that sense from her when I was in Beanies before at White Cap. Maybe driving at hellhound speed across the country had been a blessing for more than one reason.

I put my foot down, tearing a trail through the pristine snow, and wondered how many miles I'd make it down the highway before the snow chains failed me.

Not too far, as it turned out. I pulled up outside of *Beanie's,* my truck crusted in mud and slush that wasn't entirely dry. Apparently only the top third of the drive into town required snow chains, though from the clouds gathering to the north, we might have more luck on the way back, providing the slush didn't transform into black ice as the chill set in for the evening.

A truckload of young men hung over the back of a white pick up — I thought it was meant to be white — that had seen better days. I eyed them as I locked up my own truck, half hoping they were the crew Suzy had put together. The other half of me wondered if my truck was safe.

"Archer!" A familiar shape jumped down from the bed of the track and stumbled on the landing. The cowboy managed to catch his hat before it tumbled to the ground, displaying a head of rusty brown hair and a cheeky grin. The entire five foot ten inches of Will Kirk barreled forward, clapping me on the back, then Jude.

The stocky foreman straightened, otherwise not reacting to the newcomer's presence. He tilted his head down to obscure his face.

I turned back to the compact ball of enthusiasm that bounced beneath his habitual Stetson, noting the lean muscle Red Hart's prospective rodeo rider had developed. "Can you stay on a bull yet, Will?"

The cowhands on the truck bed hooted and cheered, raining shit on the poor lad.

"Not yet, sir." Will's grin turned rueful, his eyes crinkling as he took the ribbing with good natured humor. "Mighta got myself a place on the circuit though. Heard you needed some help?" Bright eyes turned concerned.

Jude coughed into his fist. "Will Kirk spent a recent season at Red Hart, Archer. He... stepped up and filled my role while I was absent from the property."

I eyeballed Will. "There's a lot of that going round at the moment."

"Stepping up or absent?" Will asked, staring me right back in the face."

I huffed a laugh. "Damn, kid. I'm glad you're not in Texas, otherwise you'd be stealing the desk out from under my best Rangers."

"Not you, huh?" Will tilted his head to one side, his dark eyes missing nothing.

My grin never faltered as I returned his study. I'd been away for a whole lot longer than I thought, perhaps. In that time the kid who wanted to ride a bull not only fulfilled that dream, or was on the way to doing it, had taken the reins of his own life and grown up in the meantime.

"Will carried Eve out of the fire up on the ridge line about a month back, wasn't it?" Jude cut in.

Will rolled his shoulders. "Maybe six weeks or so," he acknowledged. Before the snow set in. I took Cassie back to college."

I raised both eyebrows. "Shit. you got yourself a girl and you grew up? I'm fucking old then."

Jude snorted. "Are you driving this lot up, then?" He nodded toward the truckload of rowdy men ready to fill Red Hart's big house with noise to drown out Eve's borrowed workers.

I couldn't wait to ship Black Hill Boy's smell off my girl's land.

"We're all ready to work, for you Jude." Will nodded once.

A year ago, I would have expected the kid to bounce on his toes. Today he stood still, waiting for orders.

Jude cracked a rare smile. "Shit, no. These men are yours. You bring 'em in, you train 'em to work your way. That means how they behave at the house and on the land also reflects on you, kid. Got it?"

Will looked disconcerted for a fraction of a second before his shoulder straightened. "Yes, sir."

"Good. Follow us back in ten." Jude looked sideways at me. "You know Eve will want her coffee beans even if she didn't ask for any."

"I'm on it." I headed into Beanies, searching for Suzy.

The cafe owner was nowhere in sight. I inhaled a lungful of cinnamon and gingerbread. My nose itched as I weaved my way between patrons and came up with a pair of flavored lattes.

"Those aren't mine," I said politely.

"Sure they are!" Suzy popped up out of nowhere, I swore. Or at least, out of the crowd. "Eve'll love you forever if you take her one of these."

I collected the steaming gingerbread spiced lattes in careful hands. "I'm sure Jude will appreciate the effort."

Suzy's face fell. "She didn't come with you, Ranger?" Her tone came out accusatory.

I held her aquamarine gaze that sliced through me, but it was nothing that I hadn't already asked myself.

"No."

The coffee shop owner huffed out a breath as the conversational level insider Beanies swelled to a whole new level. "Alright, then. It looks like I might get to make a trip up to the ranch for Christmas morning, then, whaddya say?"

I grinned. "I say she'll appreciate the surprise. Especially if you top her coffee habit up."

"Done and done." Blue eyes twinkled back at me, almost hiding the older woman's concern. Then she was gone again, disappearing into the flurry of customers. Her voice called out, though I didn't see her again as I waded through clamoring coffee fiends to find the door.

A moment later I burst back into pale Montana sunshine.

"You survived." Jude liberated one of the spiced lattes with more enthusiasm than I expected.

"I wouldn't have taken you as a coffee snob."

He shrugged. "I married a girl with decent taste. What can I say?"

"It changes you, huh?" I gave Will Kirk a wave, and he organized his truck full of boys to follow us as we headed out of White cap and back up the range.

Jude was silent for a few minutes, concentrating on the road. "It does. In the best ways."

I hoped to hell that Eve would give me the chance to find out what that looked like for us, but as we headed back toward Red Hart, the doubts that had remained at low level for so long began to clamor.

And I could no longer keep their volume turned down.

CHAPTER 7

ARCHER

"Bunk house?" Jude made the offer in a clear voice after dinner that second night at Red Hart.

I nodded, my boots already on as the rest of the ranch hands filed along the path leading to where they all slept well away from the big house. Recalling Natalie's face when she said he refused a place in the homestead and bunked with the rest of the workers, I grinned.

"Happy to. Let me get my kit." I grabbed my bag from the back of my truck. I hadn't had a chance to unpack the night before when my only focus had been Eve. But now, a cold shower and a fresh change of clothes sounded just fine.

I ran my fingers over the mar in the paintwork of my truck, baring my teeth. If I ever found evidence of who had done the damage, there would be hell to pay, I swore.

"Archer. Catch." Eve's voice drilled through my reverie.

I swung around in time to avoid being nailed in the head by a set of keys. Flipping them over in my hand, it took me a second to recognize them. *The cabin.*

The one I stayed in last time I was here. Huh. Maybe she wasn't so pissed at me after all.

I raised my head, a simple, "*Thanks,*" on my lips, but the solitary work died a fast death as a figure dressed all in black embraced Eve on the veranda. My blood boiled as I identified the man as Joe Brunel, but the height was wrong. The figure straightened, and there was no mistaking that lean build.

Pierce MacQuaid.

Black Hill Boy.

My teeth clacked as he rested his hands on Eve's waist, and she responded, talking to him softly. Her hands rose, brushing at his shirt as he laughed softly at something she said.

Get a grip, ranger. That girl has a life you clearly know nothing about.

But damn if I didn't want it to be my business.

"Pierce's been around most nights that I'm here.

You're lucky you got one without him ruining your peace." Jude stood beside me in the darkness.

I dragged the heel of my boot through the dust, considering how furious Eve would be with me if I laid out Black Hill Boy in her front yard for no decent reason apart from the fact that he was still breathing.

"Fucking stalker, aren't you?" I said conversationally to Jude.

"I do my best."

I huffed a sound that could have been derision or a snort but that sure as fuck wasn't a laugh.

"You need help finding the cabin?"

Pierce kicked off his boots, catching Eve's hand as she held open the door. She looked over her shoulder at him, a question in her face. For a moment, her gaze flickered to mine, then she stepped inside and he followed her.

I slammed the tailgate of my truck closed, the sound echoing across fields.

"No. I remember the way."

THE NEXT HANDFUL of days ran the same way. I rose before the night began to lighten into an indiscriminate purplish haze that cast shadow over everything. Jude met me in the yard each day without fail before anyone else was up and about. His face was a mask, or maybe the frigid mornings made him grumpier than usual. My own state of mind was a different matter.

For the first few hours, we didn't talk, digging out from a fresh overnight deluge of snow to the steps and a path to the vehicles, moving the herd from barn to field as needed. The smaller ones, birthed late in the season, became stronger as Christmas approached. Eve's lost doe from the day I found her fast became a pet who followed me everywhere I went.

Jude refused to let me fall into my thoughts. We toured the fields, checking the boundary lines, ensured the animals had access to water and feed. On the rare occasion I saw some of Joe's men up near the mountain, but when I asked Jude about them, he just shrugged the question away and went back to work.

Our two groups rarely crossed paths except for at meal times, and even then we remained apart like two new herds orbiting each other, sniffing out the new threat.

Will Kirk worked his extra team hard. I wasn't sure when the kid grew up while I wasn't there, but Jude needed to watch out for his job, or maybe that was the point. One of his workers, Odin, put in the hard yards but gave him grief at the same time.

"Watch him," I murmured to Will as we set the tractor right side up that had slipped into a hole none of us swore had been there a moment before in an attempt to clear the side of Red Hart's long drive. "He sounds like he's a bag of laughs, but he'll sabotage the authority you develop with these boys overnight if you get too friendly."

Will let out a grunt as the tractor bounced a little. "Back the fuck up," he yelled, waving one hand over his head in a circling motion as he watched the ground beneath our feet, but nothing moved, thankfully.

He wasn't the only one watching. I gave Jude a sharp nod. The foreman climbed into the tractor, starting the engine.

"This ain't a rodeo," the new ranch hand in question called back to a chorus of snickers from Will's team.

"Cause you last eight seconds for anything," Will muttered under his breath as he cleared a shrub jammed under the tractor's rear tire and sent Jude a thumbs up. "Hell, honey, if you want to go a few rounds, I'll give it a try. But usually I prefer blondes with a whole lot more in the bust area, you know?" He looked up and shot Odin a saucy wink.

The older ranch hand stared at Will for a moment, then burst out laughing.

I hid a grin as I directed Jude out of the mess we'd made of the already slushy drive and prayed no one needed to use it for a day or more, seeing as we were already perilously low on salt. Maybe I shouldn't have worried about Will. The kid could clearly handle himself.

"Thanks, Archer. There's always some bully or asshole who thinks the little guy is the one they can pound down on." Will rolled his shoulders and neck, looking up at the sky that threatened to close in on us overhead.

I considered him for a long minute, doubting that anyone would be pounding down on the barrel chested cowboy before me. "Sounds like you've had plenty of firsthand experience."

"I've clocked the hours."

"Then you know how to manage him. Ignore the age difference. He'll keep testing you. Give him boundaries."

"Just like a toddler, huh?" Will's eyes sparkled at me.

"Just a like a toddler."

My daily wisdom thus imparted, I made my way back to the big house, following Jude's tire tracks.

THE FOURTH MORNING I stayed at Red Hart Jude met me at the barn holding the reins to two behemoths. I had little contact with Eve apart from collecting my coffee at the kitchen bench in the big house after breakfast along with everyone else. She barely spared me a glance when I thanked her quietly, but each morning she pushed my thermos across the bench and held my gaze with that same unreadable expression.

Like she was waiting for something.

And each day I waited for her to let me in. Because after what happened the last time I kissed her, there was no way in hell that I'd risk breaking her unspoken rules.

And so I stared up at a tall, black horse, and hoped to God that Jude didn't want me to get on it.

Thankfully, the foreman passed me the reins to a chestnut mare. Mounting easily, he turned his horse before I could question his sanity and disappeared into the pre-dawn darkness.

Grumbling under my breath, I gripped the reins in my gloved hands, pulling myself up. I succeeded, but there was little grace in my actions and I was glad for the cover of a cloudy morning that left us in a haze of ambiguous light.

By the time I caught up with Jude several paddocks later, my ass was numb and the horse and

I had developed an instant mutual dislike for each other.

"Damn good thing you've been driving a truck. Especially when you were playing at being a cowboy in front of Eve last Christmas." Jude nodded to me. "That was fucking abysmal, Archer."

"I never said I was a cowboy," I groaned, attempting to stretch one leg over the horse, but nothing cooperated. Or coordinated. With a mammoth effort, I hauled my ass myself down. The horse whickered, sidling away from me.

I didn't blame it.

"Good to know you're human." Jude watched me with his arms folded across his chest. "You over it, yet?"

"Over what?" I asked with my back to him. We both perfectly well knew what. Or maybe *who*.

A hand clapped me over the back of my head.

I winced, biting my tongue. "Damn, man." That was usually my move reserved for younger Rangers. I turned to stare at him. But a smile cracked my grumpy-ass facade when Jude's weather lined face didn't so much as shift. "No one's been brave enough to do that in a decade."

"A century is more like it. Up here, you're just a man, Archer. Not a hot-shot Ranger. Just you."

I grinned. Oddly enough, I liked that step down

a little too much. Maybe Montana suited me after all.

Jude nodded to me, his point made, and gestured toward an upturned water trough.

"How the hell did that happen?" I studied the giant contraption that looked like a behemoth had turned it on its head overnight.

Or that someone had wrapped a snatch strap around the entire piece of hardware and hauled it off its struts with a truck. The damage was colossal, the weight of the trough filled with water more than any one man could turn over without assistance. Or half a dozen.

I walked around the area, glad the horses hadn't trampled the ground too much. Sure enough, dual tire tracks started a few dozen yards back from the disaster zone. I'd bet last year's salary that I could match those tracks to one of the trucks in the big house yard. *No free guesses on which one.* I slipped my phone out of my pocket and snapped a few quick photos.

"No idea." Jude ignored me, intent on the work to be done, not how it happened. "Gotta be fixed, though. You ready?"

I had no idea how we'd make it work, but I was up for the distraction rather than worrying about Eve back at the house on her own for one more day.

"Let's do it."

My muscles screamed as I helped the stocky foreman push the trough that must have been a hundred years old, weighed down with what looked like Travis's personal brand of innovation. Overall, the work was good, and I was glad to put my excess energy to use somewhere other than moping. By the time we were done the trough was dented, much the worse for wear and empty, but back in its place.

All evidence of the tracks I'd photographed before had been erased, and I was glad I'd taken notice when we first arrived. The trough hadn't pushed itself over, and I'd been on this land the last time someone tried to sabotage my girl, hurt her and her kin. Sure, the work was a nice distraction, but my mind was never far from Eve.

Maybe I've waited long enough.

.

CHAPTER 8
ARCHER

E ve refused to speak to me at breakfast, and I wouldn't stop work during the day to flirt with her. That left evenings, with a small window when everyone left for the night.

Before Black Hill boy arrived.

I still didn't know what his game was with my girl, and I wasn't sure I wanted to know. But he wouldn't get another night with her if she objected.

My trust with Black Hill had never been a strong point. And though I had little to base that on apart from a gut feeling, I'd lived that same feeling for the last twenty something years as first a cop then a Texas Ranger.

And I could count on one hand the amount of times that it had steered me wrong.

"Whiskey?" I rose from the long table, my plate in hand as I held out my other for Jude's.

He looked up at me, considering. "Not tonight," he said after a moment. "Feel like I might turn in early." He looked aside at Will Kirk. "You up for an early night, kid?"

Will stared at his half drunk beer like it might magically evaporate, and sighed. "Guess I do, then." He took a long drink that didn't quite reach the bottom and clapped Odin on the shoulder. "We're done here."

The man looked up from his chatter. "No, I'm not."

Will hauled him up physically from the table with one hand. The chatter fell silent.

"Yes, you are. Early morning. Move it. Unless you're walking back to White Cap at the end of the season."

That little move had most of the ranch hands moving their behinds, finishing up their drinks with less class and more ass than Will, but move they did.

"Not bad," Jude murmured, stretching his shoulders.

I watched Odin, who sank back into his seat, and raised my eyebrows at Will. *There's your problem child.*

Will nodded, running a hand through his hair. *I know.*

"What if I want to stay on at the end of the season? Seems there's decent pickings here." Odin leaned his elbows on the table making a show of taking his time finishing his drink.

His one mistake? His sights were set on Eve where she cleaned up the kitchen alone.

Will sent me an easy grin as he passed me with Jude. "This one's yours."

I coughed into my fist. "Decent delegation skills."

"Told you he leveled up." Jude slung an arm around Will's shoulders in a show of support, leading the swarm outside, until there were just the four of us left in the house.

Odin watching Eve. Joe watched Odin and me with a speculative eye.

"Well, as much as I'm sure this will be fun, I like my paycheck. So...I'll see one of you in the morning." He smiled.

I didn't. "Bye, Joe," I said softly.

He stalled next to Odin. "I'd take the out he gives you." Joe patted the heavier man's shoulder, but the seated ranch hand never so much as budged, his eyes still fixed on his prize like he never heard a word.

I needed to have a chat with Jude about letting the hands drink every damn night. Maybe every second. It might cause a mutiny, but this season we had enough problems.

"Do you want to do this here, or outside?"

Joe disappeared discreetly as Odin finally turned his attention to me. "Do what?"

I shrugged, propping my ass on the edge of the long wooden table that sat beneath Red Hart's magnificent antler chandelier. "I mean, we can do this inside, but it'll make a mess. I've got some things to say to Eve after, and I don't want to waste time cleaning up." I unbuttoned my shirt, conscious of Eve listening to our conversation, making sure my voice was loud enough to fill the suddenly empty space that I'd engineered.

Odin frowned at me. "Hey, I didn't mean anything by that, you know."

I nodded. "Sure. The comment about staying on another season so you can screw with my girl. That one?"

Odin's mouth opened and shut in quick succession.

I offered him a faint smile. "I didn't think so." I dropped my shirt on the bench seat, holding his gaze. I might be a handful of years older than the man still seated at the table and apparently collecting his jaw from the floor, but I worked my ass off to keep up with the younger Rangers who entered the unit each year. My theory had always been that if I wanted to lead them, then I had to match them at the very least.

And matching anyone had never been my strength.

"Yeah. I got it." Odin shoved his plate away and stood. His height left him a few inches taller than me, but at nearly six feet I was no slouch.

"Outside is better," I murmured, holding my ground.

Odin glared at me for another minute, then stormed away. The door to the big house slammed behind him.

I shook my head, gathering the leftover plates. The kitchen was empty, and I finished cleaning up alone. *Damnit.* I knew better than to show pony around Eve. She hated every inch of it. Subtle and snarky was more her style.

Finishing up, I wiped down the enormous bench that ran the length of the kitchen and stacked the dishes in their places.

"I'm impressed you remember where everything goes." Eve appeared from behind the divider that led into the larger living room on the other side of the pantry. The windows there looked out into the foothills of the mountain behind the house. At night the outlook would be pitch black, but the light to my cabin would be visible off to the east, the bunkhouse in the opposite direction.

Maybe that was why she put me there in the first place.

"Smart girl," I murmured.

"That's not the usual response to that comment you know." Eve placed a bottle of whiskey in front of me. "Share?"

I pulled a pair of glasses out from a nook beside the fridge. "Always."

The faint smile that curled the corners of her lips left me aching for her.

"You lost your shirt," she observed, her gaze sweeping over me. Somehow her study meant more than Odin's pithy assessment.

I breathed shallowly. "What do you think? Am I too old for you, Eve?" I asked softly, the decade's difference in our ages having always been a sore spot for me.

She shrugged. "I've never really cared how old you are, Rhys. Just how much of an asshole on occasion. Come on."

I blinked. "Ouch."

Her laughter led the way through the house to the living area on the other side. She'd left the lights off, the kitchen providing an ambient glow.

"Have you always been so vicious, or did I not notice last time?" I grinned as she tossed my shirt at me.

"Put that on. Don't button it up," Eve instructed me. Her eyes dark voids in the shadows.

I pulled my shirt on, leaving it open like she commanded. "Is this a game of reverse poker, then?" I raised an eyebrow in challenge as she poured a double finger of whiskey for both of us. Honey and peat scented the air.

"I like the view." Eve curled at one end of the two seater sofa, one leg tucked beneath her, facing me. Her gaze soaked in everything as I stilled beneath her study.

"I have questions," I murmured.

"It's the cop in you. It's a habit that'll pass when you retire."

"You're still a sassy little firecracker." I sipped the whiskey and nearly groaned. "Shit, eve. This is good."

Her lips turned up in a full, wicked smile. "I know." She took her own sip, her eyes falling closed as she appreciated the flavor. "It was Dad's favorite. I figure he won't mind if I share it with you. He liked you, you know."

I swallowed hard. She wasn't the only one who struggled to talk about that Christmas. "He was a good man. His judgement might have been a bit shitty if he approved of me though." I let a man into his home who did unspeakable things to his family.

Len Beaumont should never have trusted me. Neither, perhaps, should Eve.

"Stop that." Her voice whiplashed around me.

Cool fingers gripped my glass, tugging it free of my grip. I gave in, letting her have it.

Tell me what you want, Eve.

"What's Black Hill Boy do here each night?"

Eve frowned as she placed my glass on the Blackheart sassafras coffee table. "I— Rhys, his father did a little while back. He comes here because I know how he feels."

He comes here because he can poach on your feelings like an emotional fucking vampire.

"If he needs support, maybe he should seek professional help," I said recently.

She toyed with the whiskey glass. "I suggested that. But out here, we're a long way from everything. You know that," she reproached me.

"I also know you have decent internet thanks to

the satellite connection you both paid for. Remember?" I fixed her with a hard look. Eve said nothing. I sighed, raking my fingers through my hair. "Eve, I'm here. I want to be here for you. And seeing you with other men—"

"You're jealous?" she hushed, her gaze sliding up to meet mine.

I stared at her, my mouth forming words that refused to come out right the first time. I put my thoughts in order as I reached across the table and captured one trembling hand. "Damn right I'm jealous, girl. The only hands I want on you are mine. The only man near you should be me—if that's what you want." I watched her reaction, the doubts flaring free. Fuck, I was so out of practice with this. But hell, it was Eve. I shouldn't have to worry.

But I did. Because she was my one, and there wasn't anyone else for me, ever.

"I wasn't sure." Eve tugged her hand free, wrapping her arms around herself.

"About what, honey?" My heart clenched tight in my chest, bleeding fresh with every word that fell from her soft lips.

"That I was who you still wanted. That you hadn't found someone...else. Someone who could give you—"

"*Evie.*" My voice strained on her name.

"More. A family," she whispered, curling into a ball at the other end of the sofa.

I launched forward into her space, pinning her in, but my hands when they framed her face were soft, cradling her like she was glass. The most precious creation.

"Do you know what Will did when he brought you out of that fire?" I demanded, my voice harsh and rough, the softest I could make it. She shook her head, trying to free herself but I refused to let her look away. "He gave me you, Eve. Everything I want in this life. The woman I need, the woman I'll do anything for. Anything," I whispered, stoking her temples with my thumbs. "Christ, I'm so glad you're alright."

"But I'm not." Her voice cracked as the flood gates finally, fucking *finally* opened.

I cradled her to me, weathering the torrents that shattered against my chest like waves upon a rock in a storm laden sea.

I held her until she cried herself out, my shirt damp with her tears, and mine. My fingers tangled in her hair.

And this time when I picked Eve up and carried her, it was to the sofa in front of the fire in the living room, a place where I'd slept with her once before.

I tucked us together beneath a blanket, the fire

still filling the fireplace, knowing it would see us through until morning. Because right now, that was what mattered.

Just one more night together. And Eve held on, never letting go.

Not once.

CHAPTER 9
ARCHER

"You get coffee and a kiss." Eve woke me before anyone entered the big house with her sassy as fuck lips on mine.

"Hell, girl. If that's what you're offering, maybe I should be getting down on one knee." The comment slipped out and froze us both.

Eve stared down at me, her bed mussed curls dangling over her shoulders to pool on my chest. One slim, denim covered thigh straddled either side of my waist. "Easy, Ranger. Someone's going to think you're in love." Her fingers trailed across my collar bone and lower.

I sucked in a tight breath as she reached my belt. "Maybe I am."

Her slap to my torso elicited an *ooff*. "Maybe you're thinking of something else."

My hands closed on her waist, squeezing gently. I let her see my smile before I rolled us, pinning her beneath me. She cussed me out until my mouth found hers, then her feral words turned into softer sounds that went straight to my cock.

"Rhys, the boys. They'll be here soon." Eve pushed at my shoulders, straining around me.

"Good. then maybe they'll get the point and back the fuck up," I grated, finding her mouth again. I kissed her until she moaned, her legs wrapping tight around my hips, her body rising to meet my grinds against her.

"Rhys, please. I need—" Eve scrabbled at my belt, her need rising with mine.

The door rattled. I caught her wrist, squeezing a brief warning as the door swung open.

"Jesus Christ. Can't you two go upstairs to fuck around?" Jude groused to himself as he crossed the open living space to the kitchen. "Count to twenty."

"Why?" Eve didn't move from her hiding spot beneath me, her hands tangled in my open shirt.

"Because that's how long it's going to take for Will's crew to get in here."

"Shit." Eve scrambled out from under me, taking the blanket with her.

I laughed, catching her chin and drawing her in for a hard kiss before she dashed away to hide in the pantry. I was left on the sofa with a cold ass, bare chested and no girl but laughing all the same. My shirt was buttoned—mostly—by the time Will and Odin walked into the big house. Apparently they'd made up overnight, though by the curious look Odin cast in my direction, we weren't on the same grounds.

I shot him a hard smile as I raked my hands through my hair as Eve appeared with a giant thermos of coffee, her hair twisted into a messy knot on top of her head.

"Aren't you wearing—" Will started.

Jude clapped the younger man on the back of the head. "Keep your eyes on the ground," he barked gruffly.

"My mistake." Will coughed, his face red, though whether that was from being reprimanded or for catching Eve out, I couldn't be sure. He studied the bar as the house filled with raucous chatter.

I took the thermos from Eve's trembling hands that hid nothing, pouring the coffee she'd made into the smaller travel mugs that Jude provided. Eve shot me a panicked glance and turned to cooking. Sweet maple bacon scents drifted across my taste buds and left my mouth watering but that wasn't what I craved this morning. I watched her for a long moment, knowing I wasn't the only one with my eyes on her, waiting until I was sure we had a full house.

Then, as Eve passed me, I slid an arm around her waist, turned her to face me and covered her mouth with mine. My girl tasted as sweet as Christmas morning but nowhere near as innocent. And somehow, that made the treat all the better.

The kitchen erupted in cheers as I drew back an inch, letting her breathe.

"Rhys?" Uncertainty crossed her face, though her gaze never broke from mine as she steadfastly ignored the crowd and focused on just us.

That had always been her rule: never let anyone see us together. The unspoken ranch rules.

No affection at the table.

No kissing in front of her brother.

No ranch hands upstairs.

I never had been sure which of those were her rules or just house rules that developed over time but in the last year I'd broken all of them for her.

"It's easier if they know, honey," I said softly, loud enough for her to hear me, but no one else.

Eve pressed against me. A tremor rippled through her. "Alright," she whispered back, tipping her head back.

Uncertainty still swam in her eyes, something else there too.

A plea.

Don't leave me again.

And hell, there was no way I'd abandoned my girl ever again.

I claimed her mouth in a deep kiss I couldn't break, crushing her against me. Eve folded into my chest, her curves fitting into all the right places.

"Hell, girl," I managed when we broke apart, panting. "I think there's work to be done for the day."

"Maybe?" she looked doubtfully at the mess the ranch hands had made of her kitchen, the open doors and the empty yard beyond. "Or maybe it's just us for the day?"

I tightened my hold on her. "I can do that."

"This changes things." A shiver rippled through her as she pushed away from me, her hands trembling as she straightened her shirt. "I've never—"

I trailed my hands over her shoulders. "One job at a time," I directed. "What do you want to get done today?"

She stopped. "Really? You want to do chores with me?"

I huffed out a laugh. "Honey, I'll spend every damn day with you for the rest of your life, if you'll let me."

Eve leaned back into my embrace as I inhaled her scent. "That sounds like a proposal, Ranger."

I pressed kisses to the slope of her neck until the tension washed from her body. "List, Evie. I know you can't spend a day in bed."

"Fussy Ranger," she cussed me, fixing more coffee as I cleaned up again.

"Firecracker," I countered, nipping the lobe of her ear.

She yelped and darted away. "I will *not* feed you if you start biting me."

"Biting is out. Noted."

Eve shook her head. "Texans. I fucking swear..."

She didn't have anything against Texans from her previous trip to my birth state from what I could tell. Maybe it was just me. I laughed, folding my arms as I leaned back against the bench and watched her fuss about, building a lunch pack for us that looked a whole lot healthier than the food she spoiled the ranch hands with.

I swore she should have a whole lot more workers than she did. The thought that she'd been sabotaged from the inside, or at least nearby, still irritated the shit out of me.

"You've got some issues around the ranch. You know that, right?" I caught her wrist as she darted by me, halting her panicked flight.

"I need to—" she sent me a shuttered glance, pulling away from me.

I refused to let her go so easily. "Evie?"

"For someone who just earned his way back into my good graces and who's on real thin standing, you've got a funny way of making yourself a good place, Rhys Archer." Eve worked her hand free, glaring at me beneath her lashes.

"I do? By protecting what you love most?" I held her stare. "Someone is damaging your property, honey. I'm trying to work out the *who* and *why* for you."

"Or take over." She whirled around, darting off in another direction.

"What?" I sidestepped, catching her on her return journey.

"Fuck." Eve tossed her hair to the side when it fell out of its messy bun.

"You think I'm trying to steal your place out from under you? I demanded. "Is that what being around Black hill Boy has done to my girl?"

She shook her head, then nodded, tugging at her hair.

I caught her wrists, drawing her hands down. Eve looked up at me, sucking her bottom lip into her mouth as I let her go.

"Maybe?"

"Maybe, huh?" *And you let that fucker into your house, tried to comfort him?* I tracked the motion with my eyes, swallowing hard as her waves tumbled free and wild across her shoulders. I forced the need to find Pierce and tear her neighbor apart aside. "That's a pretty look, Eve. But you don't get to distract me like that."

"It was an accident," she hissed through clenched teeth.

"Yeah?" I plucked the absent hairband from around her wrist, not calling her out on distracting me a second time, or her utter bullshit as she shook her hair forward to hide from me, looking at me through her lashes. *Fuck. Me. I'm screwed.* Blood roared to my cock. I dangled the hair band in front of her eyes. "This is the culprit, right?"

Eve continued to glare at me, kitten like. "Okay, so, fine. The ranch has issues. My neighbor is an asshole. Tell me something I don't know, Archer. It's not like I've had a whole lot of help." She huffed at me, blowing a small puff of her hair out of the way. "I have people who are fixing it."

"Or making it worse." I wound her silken hair around my fist, drawing her closer. "Did you know that when Pierce loaned you his recommendations, or were you just figuring it out when I arrived?"

Fucking Black Hill Boy.

The range of emotions that crossed her face would have been comical in any other situation. Right now though, no one was laughing. Finally, Eve blew out a breath. "He needs help. You're right, okay? You're always fucking right, Archer. Jude and Travis used to keep him in line when they were here And I— It's gotten..." she trailed off, spots of color rising in her cheeks.

I drew her into my space, leaving little air between us. "It's gotten *what*, Eve?"

She licked her lips. "I've had to turn him down a few times," she admitted. "He keeps asking."

I frowned. "Asking to take you out?"

Dating opportunities were thin on the ground locally, for sure. I got that. Eve was beautiful. It was one of the reasons that every male nearby insisted on eye fucking my girl, and why I kissed her in the kitchen this morning.

"Maybe asking to stay the night?" She winced.

I squeezed her waist. "And you let him in, fire-cracker?"

Eve closed her eyes. "Yes?"

"Did you fuck him?" The air evacuated from my lungs.

I fully expected that slap now. I had no right to ask when I hadn't been here in the first place.

She tipped her head back. "No."

I kissed her hard. Hard enough to walk her backwards to the bench and lift her tiny frame up against it. "Never. Fucking. Again. He doesn't come into this house and he's never alone with you. I don't give a fuck if he's dying. Is that clear, Evie?"

It was the only rule I'd ever give her, and only because I'd never trusted the man.

From the way she looked at me, she knew it too.

"Alright," Eve whispered.

I eased my hold in her hair, stepping between her thighs. "Did he hurt you?"

She shook her head. "No. Nothing like that. It just felt...wrong. So wrong, Rhys."

I kissed her again. "Good girl for being so damn strong." She shivered in my arms and I crushed her against me. "Now, tell me what we're doing for the day."

. . .

WHAT WE WERE DOING for the day included checking on that little doe. The creature seemed to have imprinted on me. Eve found that hilarious when the damn thing chewed a hole in my jeans. Not so much when she realized we weren't going anywhere without it.

"Come on. Bring your other girlfriend," she grumped at me, casting the doe a baleful eye. But even Eve couldn't stay snarky for that long. "Just because you got me all muddy and cold for a day doesn't mean you can steal my man. Got it?" She tapped the doe's nose, offering the deer a tiny handful of dried corn.

"Hey, that's too much," I protested.

She looked up at me, surprised written all over her face. "Look who's been researching," Eve approved. "Maybe I can make a rancher out of you after all."

I shook my head and dug my lunch pack out that she'd handed over reluctantly from the fridge before we left the big house an hour earlier. "Here. This is much better for you than that sugary crap," I told the undersized doe as she munched chopped carrots out of my hand.

"Fucking women hanging off you," Eve muttered.

I grinned. "Jealous, firecracker?"

"If she ends up in your bed, I am out."

"Noted." I watched her as she sashayed away from me, her hips swaying with more emphasis than usual, I was certain.

It was nice being on the other side of that moral dilemma, if only for a short period.

I scratched the doe under the chin until she ran off too. Then I had my own girl to chase.

Eve climbed into my truck, her fingers brushing the back of my hand as I rested it between us. She'd wanted to check the boundary where I'd found her with that doe that attached itself to me once the critter drifted away, sated and full of both cuddles and food.

I had no objection, needing to work out where the excess wire came from where it should have been attached to something fixed, not wrapped about her livestock. The drive up to the place I found her all muddied and cute with a doe in her lap was quiet., but not pensive. The tension between us had shifted from tight and fearful to a different sort that neither of us seemed to mind.

The few points of contact we had left sparks shearing across the back of my hand. It took everything in me not to pull the truck up, unhook her seatbelt and haul my girl into my lap, but Eve hated being rushed. That was part of what got us into this mess in the first place.

Hell, I'd had more patience back when I first arrived at Red Hart. I let out a soft laugh as we drove, and Eve sent me a sideways peek through her hair. She said nothing as we pulled up, jumping down from my truck to meet me near the fence where I thought we might start. It was back a bit from where I'd found her beneath the ruined tree with its lightning charred trunk, but when we arrived at the place where the fence line was cut, someone else was already working on the damage.

My mouth tightened as I counted Joe Brunel's team, each with their big black trucks parked in a neat line like a preordained barrier beside the fence.

Specifically on the wrong side of the fence, parked beside the wrong landowner.

Pierce leant me some workers.

I'd had reservations then, and more now.

"I thought you gave Joe a different assignment this morning," I murmured to Eve, turning my head away in an attempt to keep our conversation private.

She shrugged and shook her head. "I was a little occupied," she whispered back, meeting my eyes with intent written all over them. "Maybe Jude did, but...I kinda missed everything, thanks to you."

"That's fair." I folded my arms. "But a distraction shouldn't cost you a day's full wages for work another man organizes on your behalf."

Eve made a kitten sound beside me, one I couldn't quite decipher as either agreement or dissent.

"I didn't expect to see you out here, Archer." Pierce watched his men work, his ass parked on the hood of one of the trucks I suspected he had supplied for the season's work as a boost in their income.

I frowned, making a note to check who exactly was paying these men and if they were double dipping. "I go wherever the lady needs," I answered him softly, not really paying attention to the spoiled landowner's son. I checked myself. Prior landowner's son. Now the heir himself, Pierce had full control of Black Hill and everything that entailed by himself.

I hoped he took better care of the property than his father had, and with a better attitude, though I doubted it.

Joe looked up from his work as a long piece of barbed wire that I remembered vividly sprang free, slicing the arm of the man beside him.

"You'll want leather gloves for that." I nodded to the freely bleeding mark on the man's arm.

"Shane. I have something for that." Eve turned back to my truck and sighed. "Wait. No I don't. Not my truck. Archer, do you—"

"In the back." I tossed her my keys. Eve rummaged around, intent on saving the man from his own stupidity in rolling his sleeves and not bringing his own first aid kit.

Instead, she ransacked mine, patching up the minor hurt and talking quietly. Joe downed tools, wandering over. I straightened, all too aware that the man never did anything casually, without a deeper purpose.

"Pierce mentioned that you traveled all the way across the country to be with the lovely Miss Eve," Joe folded his arms across the fence post, leaning into Eve's side of the property. His greasy hair dangled across his face.

I doubted I could keep the dislike off mine.

"Did he?" I clenched my teeth.

Pierce smiled with his own brand of slimy as he observed our exchange, keeping one eye on Eve and his other man.

"She's a beautiful woman," Joe continued, as though Eve wasn't there to hear, or that worse, he thought the words a compliment. "You're blessed to have found each other. Such love is a rarity." He nodded to Eve, pushing away.

Joe disappeared into the knot of men who continued working as the one Eve tended excused himself without so much as a *thank you* for her efforts and joined his brethren.

Eve glanced at Pierce who reached for her. She sidled away, slipping through the gap in the fence unscathed. I slipped my arm around her shoulder, my interest peaked when he used Eve's neighbor's first name so readily. *Weren't you a Black Hill hire, Joe?* I doubted they were meant to be on a peer to peer basis.

Eve stiffened at the contact before the workers, her body jerking in a hard line. Too late I recalled her policy on sharing relationships before the staff, but hell, they'd have to get used to it, if she let me stay around. I didn't drop my arm, both of us still watching Pierce with a close gaze, half expecting him to let loose with something else crazy to screw with our day.

After a moment, Eve relaxed the slightest fraction, leaning back into me. A soft breath left her at the admission. I sent Pierce a shit eating grin. His eyes flashed as he turned away, barking orders to his crew working his land.

A slight ripple coursed through her and I wondered who she watched more closely—Peirce or Joe. The level of distrust grew with each until I knew exactly how she felt.

As we turned away, I couldn't help risking a glance over my shoulder.

Joe waved genially, smiling at Eve, who made no move to wave back. The longer I studied him, the more my gut tightened. Something about the way his smile and his eyes didn't match up left me on edge, like there was something missing in him. A connection with his brain that made him more predator and less human.

Loathe to turn my back on the man, I waited until Eve started off, disappearing between the trees as she headed back to the truck. She paused in the shadow, waiting for me with a small frown on her face.

Offering her a quick grin that I didn't feel I followed her lead, my heart jerking when the backs of her fingers brushed mine, then curled inward, seeking more contact.

I interlaced our hands, torn between the hope that the woman I loved still felt the same about me. That same emotion warred with the fear that Joe saw just how much Eve meant to me as a weakness.

Especially when I couldn't see him—either his men, or Pierce—as anything but a threat that lay far too close to home.

CHAPTER 10

ARCHER

I nside, the big house was cool and quiet when we returned. Eve scooted away from me the moment the door closed behind us, disappearing up the stairs. I let her go, knowing that people seeing us together spooked her. We'd packed the kitchen up together earlier in the day and I knew she'd want to get the evening meal on shortly, but she'd said we were up for a day of chores.

I wandered about the bottom floor, respecting Red hart's unspoken *no non family members upstairs* for once. The Christmas tree needed water. I topped up the firewood, split a little extra and topped up the rooms inside. My arms ached from swinging the axe, but in a good way. I preferred work to sitting around. Driving a desk had never been my style, but I'd done the job for the last few years, anyway.

I paused, slugging a bottle of water. Sweat trickled along my spine beneath my jacket, but I wasn't stupid enough to shuck the thing off until I was back inside. Behind me, the weight of the mountain's gaze weighed on my back. I placed the axe carefully by the split rounds I'd already cut, and turned to face the behemoth that had been there far longer than the ranch or any of the people on it.

The white capped peak was invisible behind a fluffy bank of clouds, but that didn't disguise the mountain's harsh gaze that watched me, anyway. I stood still, letting the mountain see me. We hadn't talked last time I was here. Then I'd thought I was a temporary fixture. Now that I sought something more permanent, it was time.

Travis spoke to the mountain. I knew that because Jude told me so. He had his own understanding with the presence that watched over the land Eve's family lived on for the past few generations. Len, too, from what I'd understood. Her father respected both the sense of peace and brutality that Red Hart existed on.

It wasn't in me to do anything less.

"She's been here for much longer than I have," I acknowledged, speaking softly, unclear if I meant Eve or the land Red hart stood on. "And I'm new. But I've been here before. I've seen a season here, and

I've protected those I love. I'll do it again, as many times as it takes. That's what I give."

Everything.

I'd never been much for speeches. Not even with new rangers. My unit could testify to that. I'd been fairly abrupt with my scant words of wisdom. But the mountain, with its bare face and thick foothills, offered no recourse at all.

Only a promise.

I'll be here long after you become dust in the dirt on which you stand.

The mountain's silent reply was humbling and powerful.

I stared up at it, awed rather than cowed. When the air chilled, I returned to the house, my tools packed away for the afternoon. It wasn't until I'd reorganized the entire log pile out the back and stacked my new rounds inside that I realized Eve hadn't come back down at all.

Breaking my promise about house rules a few scant hours after I made them, I grabbed the gift I'd brought in for her from my jacket and took the stairs two at a time, her name ready on my lips. My boot kicked her door open, I half lunged inside, prepared for whatever scene would greet me, and froze.

The fact that I'd just invaded the space of the woman I loved, the woman who I had scared less than a week ago by barging in without an invitation, slapped me in full.

Outside, I swore the mountain rumbled, laughing at me.

Hell, maybe I should be laughing at myself.

I leaned one shoulder against her doorway, inhaling the pine and pomegranate scent that seemed to follow Eve around every time I saw her, Mind, that had always been at Christmas, but it was something I knew I would associate with the thought of her for the rest of my life. The perfect Christmas morning.

She bent over her bed, stretching for something on the other side, and treated me to a damn fine view of the curve of her ass.

I cleared my throat before I left my perch and did something far too inappropriate.

"Eve," I stared, pausing when she leapt straight, whipping around to face me, armed with a cushion.

"Archer," she gasped breathlessly. "I didn't hear you come up."

"Yeah that's me, silent tracker and all." I grinned.

"I wouldn't know," Eve murmured, gripping her pillow tight between both hands. It strained in the middle. Her gaze was guarded, but nothing could hide the pain that seeped in from the sides, as though begging to be healed.

I frowned; I'd thought that with the extra help coming into the ranch, she wouldn't be quite so stretched. Taking a slow step into the room, I waited on her reaction. But she gave me nothing at all. I risked a second step, and another.

"You should know. We've spent some good moments together."

"Have we?" Eve looked up at me blindly, desperation creasing her brow, tightening the corners of those lush pink lips I'd dreamed of kissing for so long back in Texas.

And damning all the risks of her pushing me away to any hell, I didn't care which, I pulled her into my chest, wrapping my arms around her tight.

Eve stood stiff as a length of wood for a long moment, but as warmth transferred from my body to her colder one, she sank into my embrace, pressing her cheek to my chest.

My heart might have burst with pain or relief. I didn't bother working it out as I kissed the top of her head, catching her chin with my knuckle to tip her lips up to meet mine.

Christmas.

Eve smelled and tasted like Christmas.

I groaned as she opened to me, trying to take it

slow, but it was damn hard when her light kisses turned hotter, and she pressed closer into me. Winding my arms tighter around her, I breathed her in, reveling in the tiny mewls beneath my lips.

"This wasn't what I came in here for." I smiled against her lips to soften my words.

"I don't care, Rhys. Please," she begged.

Fucking begged.

I inhaled sharply, and claimed a lungful of her scent for my efforts, hardening me past the point of painful. Those dark lashes lifted, exposing the need in her eyes that matched her voice, and I was gone.

Well fucking past gone.

I speared my fingers through her hair, tangling her silken curls around them to tug her head back. My mouth crashed down on hers as a groan tore from my throat as I loosened my grip on my need for her, fitting her curves against me, replacing memory with present moment.

Eve lifted onto her toes, pressing her mouth against mine as hard as I kissed her. Her fingers worked at the buttons on my shirt, tugging them apart to run her hands beneath.

I gripped her shoulders a little too tight, drawing her back from me a fraction of a breath. It was all I could stand to be apart from her.

"Eve, if you start this..."

One gorgeous, arched eyebrow raised, bringing the corner of her lips with it.

"If *I* start this? Is that what we're calling it?" She swayed those Lucious fucking hips against mine, and it was all I could do not to grab her ass and pin her to me.

If all I had to do to get you to smile was turn you on, then wish granted, honey.

She scraped her nails over my stomach and lower. Pleasure obliterated all rational thought as she dragged those nails over the hard ridge of my cock. Even with the stiff material between us, I felt her contact on every hard inch.

"Fuck, Eve," I whispered, the blood already departing my brain and heading south.

Tugging her closer, I slid my hands down her back, pulling her shirt free of her jeans. Eve wriggled to assist me, still torturing me with scrapes and caresses.

"Months, Rhys," she murmured against my mouth. "Three months without you when you promised you would be here." The hand left my cock, and she slapped my shoulder hard.

"Ow, Eve." I laughed as I frowned, finally getting that stubborn material out of the way. My palms hit warm skin, and my laugh became a groan. "It's been a hard year here, too," I caught her mouth again, tracing my tongue over her bottom lips.

"You should have fucked me the first time." A hard accusation laced her tone.

Dark curls cascaded down her back as Eve arched into me, her tongue dancing against mine in light caresses that hardened me painfully.

"I'll give you that." I broke the kiss, spinning her around in my arms to hold her against me. The curve of her ass pressed against my denim encased cock distracted me as I worked my way along the row of buttons that dipped between the rise of her breasts.

Eve wiggled not-so-helpfully as the material parted. I ran my hands that had ached for her for so long across her stomach, over her lace clad breasts as she pushed into my touch. Our moans mingled in the flickering firelight, shadows dancing over her body as I explored every inch of exposed flesh.

I traced over her mound with light fingers. "I thought I might return the favor," I murmured, stroking over the seam that aligned with her clit.

Eve's head fell back onto my shoulder, cushioned by a mass of chestnut waves. She moaned, writhing against me.

"I think that goes both ways," she gasped, rubbing her ass against me.

"Damn, girl. This isn't the time to tease," I murmured into her ear, sucking the lobe between my lips.

Her low moan gave me everything I needed about her. I stroked over her denim covered pussy quickly, then slid my fingers down the inside of her jeans, already slick with her own arousal.

Eve bit off a yelp as I slid two fingers past her panties, impaling her to my knuckles. Her body clenched uncontrollably.

"Rhys," she whimpered, her body torn between the need to bear down on my fingers inside her and pressing back into my chest to escape the building pressure that I controlled in her.

Gritting my teeth against the pleasure that threatened to overwhelm me, I solved the problem, pushing her forward against the wall. My body formed an inescapable frame she couldn't escape from; my knuckles grinding against her sensitive flesh, trapped by the close denim that encased her, and my hips thrusting forward, pinning her in place.

Eve gasped, her hips working frantically to escape, but all it achieved was to rub herself harder against my knuckles.

"That's it, honey," I murmured, drawing my lips along her neck, breathing in her arousal. I trapped her harder against the wall, giving her no quarter. "Give me what I want."

Her breaths coming in erratic pants, Eve ground down on my hand, a scream ripping from her throat. Her soaking pussy clenched around my fingers as she collapsed against my body.

I tucked my fingers beneath her chin, drawing her head back to kiss her deeply.

"My God, I've missed you," I grated hoarsely.

Eve murmured something back, her breaths evening out as she leaned back into me.

Reaching around her, I undid her jeans, sliding them over her hips and gently eased my hands from her body.

The heady scent of her sex was intoxicating. I fumbled in my pocket for a condom, turning her gently in my arms to support her boneless body.

Eve stared at me with dark, dozy eyes. Her swollen lips were just one more temptation, and I claimed them again as I shucked off my clothes. Her shirt and bra joined mine on the floor.

"Rhys," she whispered, curving her palms around my face, "I never thought I would feel you like this again."

"Something about doubt, huh?" I grinned, rolling the condom over my cock. She reached out, but I batted her hands away, gently. "Not this time, Eve."

"Will there be more times?" She pressed her lips to my mouth, rising on her toes to rub her body against mine.

"God, I'd forgotten how much of a kitten you are," I groaned, willing an impossible effort of self-control forward. "I'm here, Eve. I'm here to stay, if that's what you want."

"If I want?" she squeaked the words, and I readied myself for another slap. "Are you fucking mad?"

Instead, Eve pressed her body flush against me, every curve exactly where it should be. The ghost I had fantasized to when I only had my hand for company faded was replaced with the real thing. Hot, soft and willing in my arms.

I traced over the curve of her hip, catching her knee when she hooked it against my thigh.

"Don't go slow," she whispered. "Please, Rhys —" Her whisper was strung out in a long cry as I drove into her.

The warmth of her body, having her so close nearly ended me. Sliding my hand beneath her fine round ass, I pressed her against the wall, holding her weight balanced over my hips.

"I've wanted you for so long, Eve. Fuck," I groaned, capturing her gaze. "You're sure that's what you want, honey? I can take you slow, or make the walls shake."

"It was my legs that shook last time," she murmured dreamily, tilting her head back, staring at me through those burnt cinnamon eyes that stole my soul. "Why don't we start there?"

My mouth crashed against her soft lips before she could finish the last word. I slammed into her, taking her air as I gave her every part of me that had desired her so much that it had consumed me for the last year.

Her bitten off screams drew me higher, tearing away the constraints I had tethered myself with, functioning day after day, all the while craving her. Digging my fingers into the soft flesh of her ass, I did as commanded. Eve's legs trembled as her pussy clenched on my cock, her hips bearing down as I pounded into her.

"Rhys, I'm coming—" she breathed against my mouth.

"And you'll fucking come for me all night, fire-cracker," I growled pushing my tongue into her mouth. I promised her that her legs would shake. I didn't mean just for five seconds while she drenched us both with a fresh slick.

Her scream muffled against my chest as I fucked

her into the wall, relentless. Every moment of panic, every fear I experienced I railed into her. Eve clung to me, those fine hands scraping at my shoulders. I'd bear her marks if it meant she was mine. And after tonight, I'd never let her go again.

The shiver that preceded her orgasm started low in her body. I pounded deeper, searing my scent into her flesh.

"Mine," I rasped against her mouth. "You've always been mine, Eve. Since the first time we were together."

Her eyes struggled open, the sight of her straining for me so fucking perfect and stunning I wanted to fill her to overflowing. But first she needed to strangle my cock a few more times before I'd let her down.

"You're mine too," Eve whispered as her eyelashes fluttered. Her feral cry as she came with those words barely off her lips sent her over the edge.

I gripped her hips tight, pulling her as deep onto my cock as I could fit her. My balls brushed the curve of her sweet, tight ass as she bore down on me, her pleasure gushing over us both.

"Fuck, Rhys," she whimpered, riding me. "I need—"

"More, honey," I promised, holding her in place

as I ploughed back into her tight, stunning body. "I'll give you everything you need."

Her scream this time was a little less feral, a little less constrained. The sound ricocheted around the room as her legs trembled around my waist. I came with a roar, her name on my lips as I damp seared my mark across her flesh.

Mine. No one else's. Ever.

"I love you, Eve." I doubted she was awake enough to hear it as I brushed damp strands back from her face. "You're so fucking perfect." I kissed her lips as she curled into my arms, her slick and mine dripping from her thighs.

I traced my fingers across her soaked flesh, gently teasing her swollen sex. "Once more for me?" I murmured, unwilling to let her up just yet.

"Again?" Eve trembled in my arms. "Rhys, you're fucking nuts."

"I know, honey. And I'm going to tease the hell out of you every damn night." I pressed a single finger inside her, the filthy feeling of our mixed fluids gushing from her leaving her arching beneath me. "Will you come for me once more?"

"I—" She panted for me with wild eyes as I stroked a slicked thumb over her clit.

"Eve?" I said in warning. "Make up your mind." I

stopped playing with her clit, stopped stroking her and left my finger unmoving inside her pussy.

Eve wiggled her hips, working herself up and down fruitlessly. "Please," she whined.

Greedy girl.

"Please *what,* firecracker?" I growled.

"Please touch me," she begged prettily.

Perfect.

I worked my fingers inside her and put, toying with her tight bud, stroking her swollen walls. Eve writhed for me, mewling and crying at the over sensitivity. My own arousal spiked as I held her down, watching my cum spill across her thighs.

"Fuck, that's pretty, Eve. Seeing you soaked like that." Her body tightened fast, her spine arching. "Christ, you like dirty talk?" I circled her clit but didn't touch the tight bundle of nerves that was ready to explode, edging her until I was ready for her again. I leaned down, licking her bottom lip. "I want to coat your pussy with my cum, smear it all over you, gorgeous. Make you filthy and mine, and—"

Eve detonated. I barely need to touch her at all.

She came without me playing with her clit, one finger gently stroking inside her sopping pussy. She clenched down on me tight enough that I hardened instantly. I could have fucked her again but I kept circling her clit lazily, through the orgasm she stole out from under me, and withdrew the finger she didn't need as her pussy wept for me.

"So beautiful and so, so naughty, Eve." I smirked as her exhausted eyes fluttered open. I fisted my cock, using our fluids to give myself long, hard strokes. "Didn't I promise you something?"

She watched me and nodded, opening her legs a little wider.

I sucked in a breath, jerking myself faster. "Is this how we're gonna be together, honey? Filthy when we're playing together? I remember how submissive you were for me that first time, holding onto that bedframe for me." I circled her clit a little faster. She whimpered, her hands rising to cover her mouth. I let her, not having a spare to hold her down. "Do you remember letting me fuck you that night, while it snowed? While your brother slept in the house, and you snuck out?" She'd been well old enough to look after herself, the whole thing happening only a year ago, but he'd been an asshole about it. I loved breaking his rules with her as much as she did.

"I remember," she whimpered around her fingers.

"Suck," I whispered, slowing my hand to watch her.

She slid three fingers into her mouth, sucking

them gently. Breath shuddered from her, a question in her eyes as she withdrew her hand.

I nodded. "Go on. I want to see it."

Eve dropped her hand between her thighs, pushing all three fingers inside herself. Her cry ripped through me as I jerked my cock hard to the vision of her getting herself off. I rubbed her clit faster as her hips raised from the bed, knowing I'd barely last a minute or two.

"Archer—" she cried.

The sound was pure and perfect, and I was done, painting her perfect pussy with white ropes of cum.

She followed me a minute later, sloshing sounds finishing her orgasm as she lay back, tracing her fingers over her bald pussy. I watched mesmerized as she mixed my cum with hers, siding her fingers through the mess, then drew it down and pushed it back inside her.

"Fuck, Evie," I said roughly, pulling her closer. Our mouths slammed together in a bruising kiss.

"Thank you," she whispered as I carried her to the shower.

The heat and steam soaked through us both. I barely remembered carrying her back to bed before we were both out wrapped in each other's arms.

The way we should have been all fucking way along.

CHAPTER II
ARCHER

E ve stirred on my chest. I propped my head up with one arm, tracing the path of her wild chestnut hair with the other. Chill bit my skin where our mingled sweat dried, but I was in no hurry to make my girl move.

My girl.

Fucking finally.

She gave a soft, satisfied sigh, and snuggled deeper into my chest. The corner of her pink, swollen lips turned up.

I struggled with the concept of not flipping her over and fucking her again for far too long a moment, and finally settled on distraction instead.

"You know I didn't have this in mind when I came up here," I murmured, winding her hair around my finger.

"Wasn't it?" Eve raised her head to prop her chin on her hand, looking at me through dark, curved lashes that only highlighted the gold flecks in her eyes. "You had a purpose other than a debaucherous afternoon together?" Her lips curled up, her tongue darting out to flick across her lower lip.

I hardened beneath her, one hand pressed between her shoulder blades. I shifted, but all it achieved was to raise my arousal.

"Yes," I said, my voice straining. I cleared it, and tried again. "Can you reach my jeans? There's something in there for you."

Eve shot me a quizzical glance and reached out half-heartedly with one arm, wiggling her fingers in the air. She gave up with a groan, slumping onto my chest with no small show of theatrics. "Do I have to?"

I watched her with amusement. "Yes."

"Fine," she grumbled, wiggling further around on her belly, her head hanging off the edge of the bed, her rump curved over my hips.

I gritted my teeth. Maybe this hadn't been the best idea. Resisting the urge to smack her ass, I leaned back, and tried to count the deer in the front field.

"This?" Eve sat up, straddling me, her present in

hand. A haphazard mass of bed-head curled tumbled over her as she sat up, completely naked and utterly comfortable.

I had never loved her more.

"Mmhmm." I drew her to me, winding my hands through her mussed hair as I kissed her until I got one of those tiny noises from her that she made when she was horny.

I released her, watching her flesh creep across the tops of her breasts as she tried to regain her composure. Her gaze flicked up to me and narrowed.

Tossing a confident smile my way, Eve straightened her shoulders, shaking her hair back from her shoulders to give me the perfect view.

So perfect, I almost groaned at the sight of her. She gave a little hip wiggle to cement her paint and waved the thin, wrapped present I had brought upstairs with me.

"What's this?"

I gripped her hips, stealing her wiggling so I could speak. "Your present, honey. I...you seemed distracted. I didn't want to wait. Plus, I kinda hoped we might use it together."

Eve's eyebrows rose. "You bought me a dildo?"

"What?" I barked a laugh. "Hell, honey. I mean I'll try toys if that's what you want, you filthy little kitten." I pressed her down onto my rock hard cock, sliding her back and forth over my length, more than ready to go again. "Christ, girl. Open the damn present." I released her, inhaling long breaths to slow my heart rate. She wasn't the only one who had been teased then.

Eve gave me a wicked grin, gave another hip wiggle and tugged the tape free from the paper. The red wrapping fell away to reveal a slightly tattered book of pamphlet size, its corners worn from tiny thumbs rolling them. I rubbed my fingers together subconsciously, the memory of my childhood over-whelming me.

Her smile faltered as she turned the booklet over, tracing the creased lines where the cover had folded over the years. She flicked through the hand-written pages, silent.

I swallowed hard. "It was my great-grandmoth-er's recipe journal. It's been handed down the family line for years. Most of my family are incredible cooks, and not just the women. Da's brisket is a life changing event. The gene skipped me." My grin skewed a bit; Eve cooked the most amazing food I'd ever had, even over my grandmother's. My lack of talent in that area was limited to a high appreciation of excellent grub. "I didn't know what to get the girl who has everything."

"Everything?" Eve raised her head, tears sparkling in her eyes, tiny snow drops clinging to her lashes.

I brushed my thumbs across them, drawing her into my arms. "The ranch, the mountain. Your family," I nodded to the yard outside where a few ranch hands milled about. "Freedom."

"And you're giving me this?" She searched my face with those dark chocolate eyes, clouded with...

Doubt?

Maybe a sex toy would have been more fun, but it was time to fess up. I'd held back too much, too long. That hurt her, and it was nothing that I ever wanted her to experience again. "I'm not here for a visit, Eve. I'm here to stay. If you want me."

Eve wasn't the only one with doubts.

"If I want you?" Her laugh had a brittle edge to it that sliced at my heart.

"I don't have to stay, and I don't want to take anything away from you," I murmured, easing back a little. "I'm not here to steal Red Hart away from you. I have my own place, but that's back in Texas. You know that."

The gap between us broadened, filled with a weight of guilt I hadn't known I'd carried.

It had taken me far too long to get back to Red Hart, to get back to Eve. Too many hours working, trying to tie everything up perfectly before I left Texas for good. But nothing as ever perfect, could ever be. And now, waiting might have cost me what I'd spent sleepless months working towards.

Eve's hands gripped me firmly, her nails digging into my shoulders. "You'll stay?"

It was a half demand, half question, and all Eve.

I wouldn't have it any other way.

"I resigned my commission. In Texas," I added helpfully.

Eve's mouth dropped open. "You gave up being a Ranger?"

That never really happened, but I wasn't about to burst her bubble.

"I officially handed the unit over to Andy the day I climbed in my truck and drove here to find you."

Eve shook her head, the rest of her body as stiff as a board. "But Archer, you've spent twenty years working on your career there—"

"A career I've fulfilled and pushed as hard as I can." Nothing I said was a lie.

I'd spent as many sleepless nights in the office chasing an endless stream of cases and furthering the careers of the rangers in my unit as I had hours trying to return to Eve after last Christmas's calamity.

"—and your unit. I know Andy." She chewed on

her lip, looking at me through her hair. "He's super sweet."

I grinned at what she didn't say. Andy Matthews was 'super sweet." she'd nailed his personality. But I'd also seen the man develop from a raw Texas Ranger into an authoritarian figure the rest of the unit respected over the last few years.

"I've been trailing Andy and Ethan to take dual control. One has the smarts; the other has the heart. They're both loyal as hell. I have no doubts, Eve." I traced a cinnamon dark curl that looped beneath her ear, running my fingertip along the line of her chin to draw her mouth to mine. "But it's okay if you do."

The curls swayed from side to side as she shook her head, her lips brushing mine. "I don't. I promise. I didn't want to push you. And you're just so. Damn. Stoic!" She punctuated each word with a finger poke into my chest.

I raised an eyebrow. "Ma'am, I think you've held that stoic card yourself for a while." Winding my hand around hers where it pressed into my pec, I kissed the tips, then folded her fingers over mine and brought them to my lips. "Hard times, good times. I'm here."

Eve's forehead pressed to mine. "Stay. Please," she whispered. "And thank you. It's perfect. I have something for you, too. But now might not be the best time." A shrill giggle escaped her.

"I'm intrigued." Slipping the recipe book that held most of my family history — birthday cakes, Sunday roasts, bean and chicken lunches that Texas was raised on, Christmas feasts—onto her bedside table, I slid my hands along her back, over the curve of her ass.

"Let me go, Archer." She wiggled against me.

I let her go with a groan. "Christ, firecracker. You're a tease."

"Says the Ranger who invented flirting."

I opened my mouth to tell her I wasn't a Ranger any more, but she was gone and it was a moot point.

Laughing softly to myself, I leaned back on her bed, one arm tucked behind my head. My eyes shuttered as the exhaustion of the last two weeks of driving and working the land for her with several partial night's sleep caught up with me. I was halfway gone when something soft, then not so soft, slammed into my midsection.

"Fuck, Evie," I muttered, wrapping my hands into her hair as I caught my breath. "You sure know how to kill a man."

"Yep." She pressed a key into my hand. "Get dressed."

I squinted at her, and sniffed. "Did you just put dinner on?"

"Yep." She knelt on the bed, wiggling like a fucking puppy. "Come on."

"What are we doing?" I watched her curiously.

"Treasure hunt?"

"Uh huh." I dug about for my jeans, swiping sleep from my eyes. "Hell, I could do with a few hours. You know that?"

"Later."

She hauled me along the hall as I pulled my shirt on, not bothering with the buttons. I wrapped my hand around hers, watching her ass as she led me downstairs and around the rear of the kitchen, stopping in front of the study door.

"Ta-daa." She waved her hands theatrically.

I raised an eyebrow. "I get to be office bitch for Christmas day?" I counted backwards. "You do know that's tomorrow, right?"

Eve blinked. "Shit. Is it? Good thing I have a turkey. Or a ham. Or five. I think. Looks like we're defrosting!"

"So..." I stalled on the threshold, looking into the lushly appointed study. "Honey, desks and I really don't agree but if you want me to do book work, I can guarantee I'll fuck something up in short order." I was half joking. Business, I could do when the need called for it, providing it was paper based. Get me into a computer system, and that was where the fuckery started.

My accountant threw a party when I left Texas, and not the retirement sort.

"Your present." Eve tugged me into the room, an exasperated look on her face. "Here." She grabbed one large, over-filled bookcase by the edge and pulled.

It didn't move.

I coughed softly. "Try the next one?"

"Nope, it's this one. Sure of it." She pulled again.

I glanced at the floor, and took two steps forward. "Right bookcase, wrong side. See?" I tapped the markings on the floor with my toes. "It budges from this side." I pulled and the bookcase swung open toward me like a secret door.

A gun safe stood behind it. Eve presented me with the key.

I took it, frowning. "Evie. Are you sure?"

She nodded. "The tumbler's ruined, long ago. This kinda works."

I stuffed about with the key until the ancient lock gave up its ghost for me. I pulled the heavy door open, exposing a rack with three rifles on it.

"Travis's," She pointed to a Remington that looked like it had barely been used. "Mine," —she pointed to another similar rifle, though this one bore more marks. "And yours." She grinned at me, lifting an ancient looking Hawken double barrel rifle from the rack. "It's a lot of fun. And it was one of the last made, I think. It's been in the family forever. Now, it's yours. Merry Christmas."

I stared hard at her. "Evie..."

"It's yours, Rhys. I talked to Trav, and this is what I wanted to give you the day you said you'd stay. So, this belongs to you, now. It's part of red Hart, and it never leaves this land." Defiance glittered in her eyes, along with a challenge.

This rifle belongs here, and now, so do you.

"Then I accept." I took the rifle from her, its weight heavy but good in my hands. "Thank you, beautiful." I leaned in and kissed her gently.

"You're welcome." Her eyes sparkled with unshed tears as she worked her arms around my neck and pulled me closer. "I've waited so long Rhys," she whispered.

I swallowed hard. "I know, Evie. Can I put this down so I can kiss you properly? I don't want to offend house ghosts right now."

She giggled at me and put the rifle back into its rack, closing everything up. Then she slid the key into my pocket.

"Love you," she whispered, and slipped past me, heading for the kitchen.

I stared after her, that simple phrase nearly knocking me on my ass.

"Damn," I muttered, leaning on the false bookcase, unsure if it propped me up or if it was the other way around. "I was looking forward to that kiss."

CHAPTER 12
ARCHER

E ve pottered around the kitchen once again filled with the scent of fresh pine boughs and cinnamon that I'd come to associate with Red Hart Ranch. I leaned across the broad solid oak bench top, surrounded by a selection of glasses and liquor.

Christmas Day was the single calendar day that Red Hart didn't actively work on. I knew that, and I'd been here last year, but it still felt strange to wake up after the sun rose on a glittering field of fresh snow and not be out working in it.

Breakfast was a slow affair, the ranch hands trickling in close to nine a.m. after their one and only sleep in—and mine. But once we started cooking, Eve, Jude and myself, and everyone else started eating, the conversation started and never stopped for the day.

As soon as we made our way downstairs, Eve had set me bartending duties. That included manning her precious coffee machine. Not that I minded, but I suspected she did it to keep me out of the kitchen while she pottered and worked through the recipes in the book I had given her. Thanks to Red Hart's never depleted pantry, she could play around with most of them, though her post New Year's shopping list pinned beside the fridge grew by the minute as she flicked pages.

Watching her play, the faintest smile hinting at the corners of her lips, gave me as much pleasure as feeling her beneath me in her bed. That soft smile was worth every second of the months we'd been apart, the heartbreak that had claimed significant damage on both sides of the line. But the way she involved herself in cooking, in providing for everyone on the ranch... That alone gave me confidence in my choice to bring a contingent of ranch hands back to Red Hart.

Especially when the big house doors opened to admit the loudest person I'd seen all day shortly before dinner.

"Suzy!" Eve yelped as she dashed forward, nearly bowling the older lady over as she de-layered

Beanies owner. The White Cap fixture shooed her away, taking a seat at the kitchen bench and refused to move as I placed a tumbler of whiskey in her hands.

"Thank you, Archer. Trader you for that coffee." She hefted a bag of beans over the bench top that must have weighed a metric ton.

"You'll send yourself broke," Eve scolded her, waving to Natalie who fell in the door, covered with snow and followed by Trader Kyle and his wife, Sienna. They parked themselves at the end of their long table, well away from Joe Brunel's group who grew rowdier as the night began to set in.

Will sent me a concerned glance but I shook my head, knowing Jude would pull them into line or kick them out before real trouble brewed.

"Fresh coffee?" I offered, weaving a thermos at Eve.

She cast me a quick grin, her gaze flicking back to the recipes that she was still trawling through, making extra lists.

"Sure. I think there's some gingerbread flavoring on the bench if it hasn't run out. Watch Natalie. She has that stuff on ice cream like it's going out of fashion." Eve trailed her finger down the line of ingredients listed on the page, tapped one and disappeared into the pantry.

I glanced at Natalie who turned a shade of red and ducked away.

"Be quick with that." Jude leaned his back against the bench at my side, nodding to the growing line of ranch hands clamoring for their round of Christmas spirits. "You sure you're up for this?"

"Of course?" I shrugged. How different could pouring a stack of drinks for some thirsty ranch hands be? Surely it couldn't be worse than dealing with a staff Christmas function.

Thirty whiskey sours, a dozen beers and a vodka martini later, I had a new appreciation for bar staff.

Jude raised his cocktail from across the room, saluting me. I shot him a dirty look, though the corner of my mouth turned up.

Not bad, Ranger, he mouthed.

I snorted as I cleaned up the empty bottles, logging them to a mental itinerary. Eve's kitchen might be full, but there was a significant lack of top shelf spirits I intended to stock her cellar with.

A single glass clanked onto the bench in front of me.

I looked up into eyes so similar to Eve's, but these barely hid the shadows that still haunted him.

It wasn't only the ranch hands I was glad I had invited back to Red Hart.

"Travis," I nodded warily as he slid his glass forward. "Didn't see you come in. What can I get you?"

Eve's twin regarded me with a shuttered face for a long moment, and he nodded. "How about a damn fine dose of gratitude for looking after my sister for the last few weeks?"

Thank Christ for that.

"And here I thought I was going to find out what sort of fighter you are." I held his gaze, waiting for the other shoe to fall.

The Travis I knew from my last trip to Red Hart had been cavalier, flighty and quick to anger. After his accident and months unable to work the land he loved, this version of Travis still held a decent dose of anger simmering just below the surface, but he watched me with a sense of peace that had never been present in him before.

He tipped his head to one side—and Eve gesture that he shared with his twin. "The sort that managed to pull his head out of his ass with no small amount of pushing—*oof.*" Travis raised his arm as a tornado of dark curls crashed into his side.

"Travis!" Eve grinned, wrapping her arms around him in a fierce hug.

I'd been on the other end of enough of those to know that it had to help Travis heal, at least a little.

"Damn, babygirl. You pack a punch." Travis raised an eyebrow, his dark curls that matched hers, albeit shorter, flopping over his face as he hugged her back.

"Not yet," she warned him, stepping back. "I didn't expect to see you this year."

Travis' gaze shifted to hold mine. "I wasn't sure either."

Eve caught the look, the pain of not having her twin beside her leaking through the ether between us. She mouthed *thank you* to me, then returned to her brother and punched his shoulder.

Hard.

"Fuck," Travis muttered. "I didn't come here to be beat up, Evie," he grumbled.

"You shouldn't have waited for Archer to call your ass to come back and see me. I needed you."

"Yeah?" he grinned. "Maybe that goes both ways, little sis."

"What are you drinking?" I asked, twirling his glass between my hands.

Travis grinned. "Something terrible, from the look of what Jude's having."

I raised my hands in surrender. "Not my choice of station, my friend."

Eve slipped around to my side, burrowing into my shoulder. "Thank you," she murmured again

I concentrated on filling Travis' glass. "For what?" Eve nudged my shoulder, and I slopped whiskey. "Dammit."

"You know why." She shook her head. "I can't understand how you keep pulling miracles on me."

"I'll keep them up as long as you'll have me around. And I need to talk to you about your lack of a spirits cabinet. Decent ones, anyway. Apart from this." I held up the peat whiskey.

"So you are staying then? Really staying?" Eve's fingers grazed over my stubble, turning my face to meet hers.

I handed Travis' glass over without looking, uncaring if I dropped it on the floor. From the swearing at my side I might have, but I blocked it out, cupping my whiskey stained fingers to Eve's soft cheeks.

"I'm staying. I don't care how many times you ask, or how many times I have to say it, Eve. I'm here for you. Nothing can take me away."

She leaned into my touch with a sigh that on any other day might have boiled my blood and have me carrying her up the stairs, but for tonight with the scent of her happiness and contentment wrapped around me, all I could do was smile.

"I love you." I murmured, kissing her gently. When I pulled back, tears cascaded down her cheeks. I brushed them away with my thumbs. "What's this?"

"I love you too. I won't survive you leaving again, Rhys. I can't." She bit her lip, staring at me with those haunted eyes, so like her brother's from their shared tragedies.

"I'm not leaving, Eve. I never should have in the first place and I sure as hell shouldn't have stayed away for so damn long." I kissed her again. "Anything that comes at you, we face it together. Not alone, right?"

"Right," she whispered, wrapping her arms around me tight in the sort of hug that only Eve could give. The kind filled with healing, and hope. "I love you too."

I buried my head in her curls, crushing her to my chest.

"Merry Christmas, Eve."

"Merry Christmas, Archer."

Red Hart Ranch was once again full of the people who loved the land, and who adored the woman who ran it. I settled with my back to the wall, Eve held to my chest as Jude started a round of bawdy songs, and promised myself I would hide the damn vodka from him.

When I managed to extract myself from the

woman I'd crossed the country to find again, which might take a while.

Because in no way was I ready to let her go any time soon.

I spent more time over the next two hours cleaning than I did with Eve in my arms. A problem I'd rectify as soon as everyone left for the night, I promised myself.

"We're gonna use the cabin that I never unpacked into, right? Now that you're brother's here? Because he sure as hell doesn't want to listen to you coming all over my cock all night," I murmured into her ear as I pinned Eve top the wall in the pantry, squeezing her hips possessively.

"You can't say that," Eve hissed, her resolve breaking the moment my mouth sealed over hers.

"Hell, I can't even get a bottle of whiskey to take

to bed," Travis grumbled, walking into the pantry and straight back out again.

Eve giggled into the crook of my neck as I grinned down at her.

"So, my place?"

"Mmhm." She murmured, tracing patterns on my torso. "You know this is your place now, right?" I swore she'd perfected looking up at me through her lashes.

"Yeah. but still I don't really want to fuck you to your twin's commentary all night. And we are going all night, Evie," I growled, licking my way across her throat.

She moaned appreciatively, tipping her head back to gift me access.

"Shit. Archer!" someone called from the living area. Possibly Will, from the stifled laughter. "Your girlfriend's back."

"What the hell?" I frowned down at a giggling Eve. "You've had too much coffee."

"You made yourself a friend. She peeked around the edge of the pantry to a chorus of catcalls, waving them away as her cheeks stained a pretty scarlet. "Oh, hello."

The doe who had been following me about trotted up to the kitchen the moment I stepped out with Eve.

Now who let you in?

"Ah. Shit."

The house broke up as I sent Eve a rueful glance over my shoulder.

"Dump him!" someone yelled from the long table. Probably Joe.

"I'll be right back."

"Mhmm." She gave me a finger wave and looked at the doe pointedly. "We are having words in the morning."

"Yeah, yeah." I grabbed my coat and a carrot, busting the vegetable up into the smallest pieces I could in my hands. "Come on, honey. You belong outside. Was your gate left open?" I frowned as I slid my feet into my boots, shrugging my jacket on as I glanced over to the field adjoining the house yard.

The light barely made it that far, but the doe trotted obediently with me as I strode across the hard packed dirt. Sure enough the gate banged against the far fence post.

"Fuckers didn't latch this." I tossed a handful of carrot into the snow. The doe looked at the carrot and back to me. "Come on. In you go. Fuck." I bent down to retrieve the carrot pieces.

The doe wandered into the field, nibbling out of my hand. I sighed.

"There you go. Much better." I closed the gate,

praying she was the only one who wandered out, and how long the damn thing had been open for. Pulling my phone out of my pocket, I lit the flashlight app, but there wasn't a single deer in sight.

Shit.

Either they were all where they were supposed to be, or they were somewhere else. Biting back an oath, I jogged to the barn and grabbed a quad bike. A quick trip with the headlights running found absolutely no deer anywhere they shouldn't be. By the time I returned to the big house, most of the ranch hands were heading back to the bunk house for the night.

I grabbed Joe's shoulder. "The damn gate was left open. Know anything about it?"

He turned to me, his smile lazy. "No idea. Anything else other than your little friend get out?'

"No that I can see. That herd is Eve's pride and joy. If I find out—"

"I didn't hurt your girlfriend's toys, Ranger Rick," Joe said softly. "But if I see a pretty thing I'll be sure to call. Merry Christmas."

I let the man's shoulder go, all too ready to kick him off the land, but to be fair apart from being an asshole, he hadn't done a damn thing wrong.

I parked the quad bike in the barn, locking up for the night and headed back into the house. Exhaustion slammed me along with a decadent dose of heat from the overstuffed fireplace as I shrugged my jacket off.

"All done?" Jude called from the sofa where he sat with Natalie curled around him.

"Yeah, all locked up." I clenched my teeth, unwilling to worry him, glancing around. "Where's Eve?"

"Upstairs." Jude yawned, setting us all off.

I grinned. "Cheers. I'm done. Merry Christmas."

"No, she's not." Travis walked slowly down stairs, his limp visible as he leaned on the banister. "Eve. She's not up here. I just checked her room. She might be in the study."

My grin dissipated. "I'll check." I circuited the house, my unease growing with every step. "Eve?" I called, opening the back door. "Did she follow me outside?" I asked Jude, returning to the living area.

His tired eyes blazing with a shot of adrenaline. "No."

"Fuck."

"She'll be upstairs. Or somewhere," Natalie offered from her space on the sofa. "What?"

I looked at Jude. "Have you told her?"

He shook his head. "We haven't really gone into it."

I nodded. "Now might be a good time. After we check the house again."

Which we did, but I knew it would yield the same results. I walked straight into the study and pulled the bookcase out.

"The hell are you doing?" Trav asked from behind me as I grabbed Eve's rifle.

The one she gifted me was stunning. It was also a historical gift and an emotional piece.

Hers was useful. I'd handed in my ranger issue handgun back when I left Texas.

"It's not a coincidence." I didn't say anything else as I loaded the gun with sure fingers. "I'm going to check the cabin. Anywhere you can think of?"

Trav made a feral sound. "The cellar."

I froze. "You're fucking kidding me. I thought—"

"Yeah, well. We changed a few things."

"Make it count. Take Jude."

"He's drunk." Desperation coated my girl's twin's voice.

Not again.

"It's better than nothing." I walked out of the big house and headed straight for the cabin.

I'm not wrong.

Please don't let me be wrong.

CHAPTER 13

ARCHER

othing can take me away.

No, nothing could take me away from Eve. But I hadn't counted on someone stealing Eve away from me.

Fuck.

My footsteps quickened as I jogged toward the cabin in a crouch. Lights blared from every window, the curtains I'd left open giving me a view of a body moving within.

Please let her have gone there to prepare for me.

I still didn't walk up to the front door and knock.

Honey, I'm home. How are you doing? Being tortured and kidnapped like last year?

That's how tonight plated out. I knew I wasn't wrong.

I circled the cabin, keeping my steps light and

quiet. The snow didn't help but the slush did and so I kept to the shitty parts that let me creep up on the space where I knew my girl was.

"Here, and here, and here. That's right, isn't it, sweetie?" A male voice filtered through the night. Muted, but loud enough in the silence.

Cooing, like a lover.

He's fucking cooing at her.

"And here....no, you stay still now. No...shhh. *Shhh*, I said. *Fuck*." Something crashed over, the sound giving me an opportunity to risk the creaky steps to the short veranda.

I glanced through the window as I passed, but the dark head that obscured my view of whoever else was in the cabin gave me plenty of information.

Tall, dark, heavy set.

We had one ranch hand that fit that description. I didn't need to see his face to know who I was dealing with.

Odin.

The ranch hand who gave Will so much grief. I almost wished it was Joe Brunel. That would have been a whole lot more satisfying.

A whimper froze me where I stood before the door.

"I said hush, sweetie. That's it. We aren't anywhere near done. You hush and we keep going."

I breathed in and turned the handle on the old door. One way, and it creaked like fuck. The other way... Not so much.

Righty tighty, lefty loosey.

I just had to pick the correct direction.

Right, and the handle started to stick. *Left it is.*

I twisted and let the door crack the finest amount, shouldering the weapon. My boot kicked the door inward as I cocked Eve's gun, sighting it.

It didn't take more than a fraction of a second to register my girl curled in a ball with red streaks decorating her arms in a cruel parody of Christmas tinsel and Odin looming over her with a knife that flashed in the light.

It didn't take me more than a fraction of a second for twenty years of training to kick in and for my finger to feather the trigger.

Just once.

And it only took a second for his body to fall.

The sound of the shot echoed off the mountain long after Odin created his own Christmas decorations on the cabin floor.

But for the first time in twenty years, I didn't announce my presence before I took the shot.

I wasn't a Ranger any more.

"We're gonna burn this fucking cabin to the ground, I grate out as I laid the rifle on the sofa beside Eve, peeling her hands from her face. "Fuck, kitten. I wasn't there for you."

Tears streaked her face, mingling with red. I stroked her skin that appeared undamaged, thank fuck. But her arms...those were sliced up. I cradled her top me, cautious of the damage to her as I pulled my phone out and pressed call.

"You have her?" Travis's voice was frantic.

"Cabin. Get me a fucking ambulance. Again," I gritted out.

"Yes, sir." He hung up.

I kissed the top of Eve's head whispering soft things to her. "I'm so sorry, Eve. Fuck, I should have seen it."

"What, that your other girlfriend would be a decoy for Simon Haldon's brother?" she sniffled as she looked up at me through a fresh sheen of tears. "That's some utter bullshit right there, Ranger."

"Not a Ranger anymore, Eve. I'm just yours."

She closed her eyes and rested against me, letting me hold her until the light around us changed to flashing ones I thought I'd escaped forever.

"I know," she whispered.

EPILOGUE

ARCHER

I stood behind Eve as she spoke quietly to her parents. We'd spent the morning clearing weeds and grasses away from their graves in the family plot above the big house. The grave yard was a decent pilgrimage and we'd package a bit of food and a few other things. Eve had taken to wearing sleeveless dresses as the weather warmed. Though she was out of bandages now, I knew the thin scars on her arms still bothered her.

We had no firm idea of how Simon Haldon's brother had found Eve, but it wasn't too hard to guess. The news reported heavily on his arrest in Texas, following both of us earlier in the year when he stalked her to my place. It seemed that news had followed her all the way back to Montana, along with Odin.

I had a new job at Red Hart—vetting incoming ranch hands, the same way I used to vet rangers. Apparently I did have some useful skills after all. Everyone from Joe's crew had cleared out shortly after Christmas, and Pierce kept to his own side of the fence line. That was the way it would stay, as far as we were both concerned. Travis and Jude too, now that they understood the full story—all of it.

The doe still didn't leave me alone, following me most days. She was pregnant now, had her own boyfriend much to Eve's hilarity. We'd decided to choose a name together later in the year.

But for now, I waited while Eve had the quiet conversation she needed with her parents each month.

"I'm ready to head back, if you are?" Eve appeared by my side.

I slipped an arm around her waist, drawing her away from the grave sites to a rocky outcrop that looked away from the big house and its fields and deeper into the mountains behind Red Hart.

"Not just yet." I leaned down and kissed her gently. "How are you feeling?"

She shrugged. "Good, I suppose. Then tight. Panicky. Then I see you, and I'm okay. Then, repeat."

"It might take a while."

"If *'a while'* is a decade or so." She raised her hand to run her fingers across the garnet and diamond necklace I'd given her when she came to see me in Texas. The garnets represented red Hart, and the stars were laid out in the shape of one of the constellations above the mountain I'd loved the first time I came here.

"If it takes a lifetime, and me being here helps, then that's what we do, Evie." I stroked the back of her neck, my lungs constricting.

She shifted. "What are you up to?"

I grinned. "You should have worked in my office, you little feral."

"Uh huh. Spill."

Pressing a kiss to her temple, I extracted the small black velvet pouch from my pocket and placed it in her hands. I didn't have a speech, and I knew she wouldn't expect one from me.

Eve's sharp inhale told me she knew exactly what I was doing.

"Archer..."

"Open it."

Eve leaned into me as she undid the pouch's strings and tipped the white gold ring inside onto her palm. The Yogo, one Travis gave me a year ago, was set in the middle, the mountain behind the house carved into its surface by Bode Hunter, the artist who lived deep in the mountains we looked at now.

"This is one of ours." Eve closed her eyes. A shattered breath left her. "You had this made up, didn't you?"

I hummed. "Bode carved it for me. We talked about what would be the right thing for you for weeks. I'm sorry I didn't give it to you sooner."

She shook her head. "No. It's perfect. Thank you."

I slid it carefully onto her finger, protecting her sensitive arms. Eve looked down, and when I couldn't bear it any longer, I caught her chin between my fingers and tipped her face up.

Tears glazed her cheeks.

"Eve?" I murmured. "I'm gonna need an answer."

"You haven't asked me a question."

I smiled, leaning down to brush my lips across hers. "Do I need to?"

Eve sighed, pulling me down to her. "I'm yours, Rhys. I've always been yours."

I kissed her gently, savoring her cinnamon and gingerbread taste. "Is that a yes, then?"

Yes," she whispered, melting into my arms. Salt

mingled into our kiss, the mountain's chill wind wrapping around us, though its bite never hurt.

I'd chosen a place where the mountain could bear witness to Eve's decision, what we chose together for Red Hart, its stoic gaze lighting on us as Eve let me kiss her until her hair tangled around my fingers in a knot, weaving us together.

And then I didn't want to share her with anyone at all.

THANK YOU
FOR READING

Thank you for reading Eve and Archer's series at Red Hart Ranch. Please leave a REVIEW. They really do matter, even if it's a few words of what you loved about the book or the characters.
Read all of RED HART RANCH here.

Will Kirk gets his very own series in Ridin' Horns Rodeo. You can start the first book here with KICKING UP DUST.

Read on for a chapter from FORGOTTEN MOUNTAIN MAN.

FORGOTTEN MOUNTAIN MAN - SNEAKY PEEK - CHAPTER ONE

FAITH

"You're going up *where* in *what*?" Jude looked at my car over my shoulder and managed to suppress his laughter. "Take one of the farm trucks, please, Faith, or I'll be scraping you off the mountain when the deluge hits in a few hours." The foreman of Red Hart Ranch waved a tanned hand toward a row of dusty, branded red and white pickups parked in a neat row out the front of the big house.

I plastered a smile on my face that had wore down on much lesser men than Jude Mannering—and much less well-mannered ones, too.

"No thank you, sir," I declined politely. "Me and Pretty Betty are going to trundle on up that little hill, give our papers to one Mister Walker Roan, and be back before the sun sets."

I pointed to the manilla folder fat with a sheaf of files stuffed inside where it perched on the passenger seat of my ancient bubble car. Long overdue for replacement since I graduated college, I still hadn't upgraded my ride despite opening my own office in White cap, a few hours' drive south of Red Hart. Maybe I should after this. One last road trip in Pretty Betty for my current client.

Or rather, my late client's son.

"Are you still driving that beat up old thing, Faith? Betty hasn't given out on you yet?" Travis Beaumont, co-owner of Red Hart with his twin sister, Eve, stomped down the wide front steps of the big house, banging his black hat on his denim covered thigh. "You know a girl should spoil herself when she has her name plastered in big letters in the main street."

He leaned down from his six-foot, six-inches height to engulf me in a bear hug where I nearly died from lack of oxygen within seconds.

"Letting that same girl breathe helps," I huffed at him, slapping his shoulders with my hands on his back where I could reach.

"Oops." Travis sent me an apologetic grin. "I do

the same thing to my wife sometimes. She's almost as small as you."

I snorted. "Bet she doesn't grumble."

His cheeks pinked. "Yeah..."

Jude coughed into his fist, and the sound was fake as all hell. "Still holding to my point, Fatih. With those clouds closing in, you shouldn't be going up the mountain. Not today."

I stared at the fluffy white peaks that decorated the imposing peaks behind Red Hart's big house in a pretty ring. "I can still see the summit, Jude. Seriously?" I eyed Travis, waiting on the landowner to weigh in. Not that I didn't trust Jude, just that...

Okay, so the ranch foreman was known to be overprotective with pretty much everyone who crossed the land he considered his to protect by right. And I knew he was being a sweetheart, but he also hated leaving ranch land. I was about to cross well beyond anything that was considered Red Hart boundaries, even though I'd spend a good half hour driving right across the eastern boundary to enter the next territory.

Which was where I'd find Walker Roan. Eventually.

My client passed away over two years ago and I'd been emailing, messaging, calling and finally snail mailing his son since then to clear up the little matter of his twenty freaking million dollar inheritance that had been burning a hole right through my desk that entire time.

Anyone else would have been dying to get their hands on the patch of prime Montana land on the outskirts of White Cap. Anyone, apparently, except Walker Roan.

Now, it was time to collect, for both of us.

Walker Roan wouldn't be able to ignore me when I turned up on his doorstep. Not this time.

Travis kicked up dust bunnies with the toe of his boot. "I dunno that heading up the mountain is such a good idea, Faith. Maybe wait til one of the boys can take you. If you hold out until next week, then Eve or I can go with you. Make a picnic date of it and we can all catch up together?" Hope lit his eyes.

I hated dashing it in one.

"Not you, too?" I placed a hand on his arm. "Is this even about the weather?"

The boys exchanged glances over my head. I stomped my heel in the dirt. "Don't do that. I am *not* insignificant just because I'm a foot and a half shorter than everyone here."

Jude snorted and ruffled my hair, the sweetheart–asshole. "No, you're far from insignificant,

Faith," he rumbled. "But we worry about you. No one's seen Walker in..."

"A while," Travis put in softly. "I don't know that he's in any sort of consumable human state. Not for you. For all we know he's turned into a cactus up there," he tacked a joke onto the end of his anti-Faith-mountain-date-spiel.

A crap one.

I glared at him. "I don't need Roan to be in a consumable state. I just need him to say yay or fucking nay, sign or come back with me, and the deal is done."

"He won't come back with you," the boys chorused like twins.

I raised my eyebrows. "You two married the wrong people. Thanks for the heads up. And the coffee." I hugged Eve as she trotted down the steps holding an oversized coffee thermos.

"I wasn't about to send you off unarmed." She hugged me back and produced a container of assorted home cooked slices out of nowhere. "Plus, in case it really does close in and you get stuck. You need to turn around, there's always a bed for you here. And Kyle is about on the other side of the mountain if you need help in that direction. Not that there's any reception once you hit the boundary."

She frowned and winced all in the space of a second. Her hand dropped to her hip and she squeezed inward.

It was my turn to worry about her. "Are you okay?"

"Fine." She brushed off my concern with a tired smile. "Perimenopause hitting in five years too early. Hot sweats have started too."

I stared. "You are way too young for that. Have you been to the doctor?"

"Too many times to count. Do you have enough fuel? Got jerry cans?"

I blinked. "I hadn't thought—"

"Walker has a stash, assuming it hasn't all gone stale. Been a long damn time since he was in town," Jude muttered. "I can get you something." He eyed my trunk. "Make your car stink, though."

"No, thank you. Pretty Betty shalt not stink. The car commandments." I hefted my lunch container and my coffee thermos over my head to increase my height before the predators crowding around me and air kissed Eve. "Look after yourself," I whispered. "I'll be back soon, with Walker."

Her eyes sparkled with my impending mischief. "I can't wait."

Then I was gone in a flurry of dust bunnies bigger than the ones that Travis kicked up, headed for Red Hart's eastern boundary where I would find Walker Roan and finally get his oversized, over-stuffed and long overdue file off my otherwise clean desk.

MEET WALKER ROAN

ABOUT THE AUTHOR

USA Today Bestselling author Sofia Aves writes fast-paced police romances, sizzling military units, steamy cowboys with a Montana backdrop and the occasional cheeky god. Sofia writes kidlit for charity and has over one hundred and fifty publications across six not-so-super-secret pen names. As acquisitions editor for Evernight and Evernight Teen publishing she loves discovering new talent in romance and YA spaces, and is a mum of three crazies in a returned veteran household. Sofia has two overly large fur babies who think they're teacup puppies, a duck who prefers to eat from a dog bowl and two axolotls named after a dragon and a firebird.

Sofia lives near Brisbane, Australia, where she has her own alpaca park, Lorendel.

www.sofiaaves.com

READ SOFIA'S SERIES

Blue Blooded Brothers

Collision

Politics & Paperwork

Blindsided

Sentinel

Mugshots & Candy Canes

Impact

Reckoning
Red Hart Ranch
Snow on the Range
Siren on the Range
Sundown on the Range
Spirit on the Range
Ash on the Range
Mistletoe on the Range (2025)
Forgotten Mountain Man
Texan Devils
Ranger's Wish
Ranger Bedevilled
Ranger's Passion
Ranger's Fury
Ranger's Wrath
Ranger's Storm
Snapdragons & Seductions
Summer with a Ranger
Merry with a Ranger
Beach Duty Collection
Playing to Win
Off Boarding
Vicious Slash
Zero Pointer
Off Stage Fling
Rippton Allstars
Crushing It

Glacial Force

Rippton Creatives

Study Games

Make Me, Break Me

Twisted Obsession

Spring Break with a Mafia Prince

A Royally Fake French Menage

Angel Shot

Jericho Chimeras

Puck Me Always

Puck My Heart

Puck me Sideways

Z Boys

King

Joker

Hearts

Ace

Mayhem & Mistletoe

Ruski

Fast Track to Love

Speed Trap

Klauss Brothers

Zander

Keegan

Gallo Empire *with Jade Marshall*

Splintered Vows

Fractured Vows

Fierce Vows

Savage Covenant

Rom Coms

She's A Hot Christmas Mess

Boats, Moats and Root Beer Floats

Writing Romantasy as

SOFIA SHELLEY

Dead Poets Sorority

Writing Reverse Harem Dark Romance as

DOVE PRIEST

Recurve Ridge

Kidlit writing as

JO SEYSENER

The OCD Elf

The OCD Elf's Great Reindeer Calamity

Greg and the Egg

writing YA as

JOSS PHOENIX

Alchem Academy

HIDE FROM US

Writing spicy paranormal romance as

RAVEN HUSH

Club Fray

Darkest Desires

Purge

Kidnapped By Claws

Ruin

Shadow Lords

Sinner's End

Heaven's Gate (2026)

Monster Brides

Phoenix's Eternal Flame

Kraken's Vow

Krampus' Christmas Bride

Silent Sentinels Duet

Reflections of Silence

Echoes in the Void

Monsters In New York

Feral Moon Rising